Lynne Graham

A MEDITERRANEAN MARRIAGE

A Mediterranean Marriage

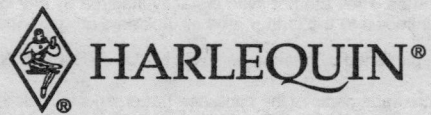

HARLEQUIN®

TORONTO • NEW YORK • LONDON
AMSTERDAM • PARIS • SYDNEY • HAMBURG
STOCKHOLM • ATHENS • TOKYO • MILAN • MADRID
PRAGUE • WARSAW • BUDAPEST • AUCKLAND

For my editor, Tessa Shapcott,
in fond appreciation of her creative support
beyond the call of duty.

ISBN 0-373-12295-0

A MEDITERRANEAN MARRIAGE

First North American Publication 2003.

Copyright © 2002 by Lynne Graham.

Visit us at www.eHarlequin.com

Printed in U.S.A.

CHAPTER ONE

WHEN his new investment consultant had finished speaking, Rauf Kasabian gazed out across the Bosphorus strait towards the city of Istanbul, his lean, handsome features grim.

For once, Rauf was impervious to the magical spell cast by his waterside home. The ever-changing play of light and shadow over the shimmering water and the gentle lapping of the tide usually relaxed him. But his bitter memories triumphed over his surroundings and now his anger had been roused as well. So, the Harris family had played ducks and drakes with his money and Lily was flying out to Turkey in person to ask for what? Special treatment? On what grounds? That her family should choose *her* as messenger had to be the ultimate insult!

In receipt of that bewildering lack of response from a tycoon whose ruthless intolerance for dishonest business practice was legendary, Serhan Mirosh regarded his employer with anxious eyes. Had he himself overreached his powers in taking instant punitive action in the affair? True, the funds involved were mere pocket change to a media mogul as wealthy as Rauf Kasabian, but Serhan took keen pride in his attention to detail. Uncovering the disturbing history of Rauf's unprofitable investment in the small English travel firm concerned had seemed a laudable effort for he had been dismayed that his predecessor should have allowed such flagrant irregularities to continue without intervention.

'That in over two years you should have earned no financial return for your backing is outrageous,' Serhan recapped with measured care, in case he had omitted some salient point in his previous explanation. 'In line with the contract you agreed with Douglas Harris, I have demanded the repayment of the original sum invested plus the percentage of profits which you should have received during that period.'

'I'm grateful that you have brought this matter to my attention,' Rauf asserted with a cool nod of acknowledgement.

Praised, Serhan relaxed and spread speaking hands. 'I cannot understand why this Harris woman should now seek a meeting with you but my faxed response to that effect and indeed my refusal on your behalf has been ignored. Yesterday I received a second request for an appointment between the fourth and the fifteenth.'

As it was now the second of the month that could only mean that Lily would soon be on Turkish soil, Rauf registered, his lean, lithe, powerful length tautening at that awareness. 'The English can be stubborn.'

'But such persistence is rude,' Serhan lamented. 'What is the point of this woman coming here? The time when explanations might have been considered is past. Furthermore, it is her father who owns the firm.'

Rauf decided not to add to the other man's confusion with the additional news that Lily Harris was, or had been three years earlier, training as a nursery school teacher. 'Leave the file with me and I will deal with it,' he instructed. 'I would also like to know where Miss Harris is staying.'

'In an Aegean coastal resort,' Serhan advanced drily, but he was unable to quite conceal his astonishment that Rauf should be prepared to give his personal attention to such an undeserving cause. 'Perhaps Miss Harris believes Gumbet is next door to your head office in Istanbul!'

'It's possible.' In a mood of rare abstraction, Rauf was studying the file that he had already opened with hard dark golden eyes. 'When I knew her, geography wasn't her strong point.'

When I knew her? A startled exclamation on his lips at that revealing comment, Serhan thought better of voicing it and departed. At the same time, he wondered how his employer would react to the discovery that Harris Travel had treated the Turkish builders engaged to build villas for them in a dishonest and disgraceful manner.

Some minutes later, Rauf cast aside the file, a cold gleam in his dark gaze, his handsome mouth clenched hard. He was outraged by what he had read: Lily would receive no mercy from him. He remembered her eyes blue as the summer sky telling him that he was the centre of her world. A cynical laugh fell from Rauf's wide, sensual mouth. Yes, he had believed her to be both sincere and innocent. Like countless men before him, in burning to possess one particular woman, he had, momentarily, shelved intelligence and caution. Mercifully, it *had* only been the weakness of a moment from which he had soon recovered.

But then, long before he had met Lily, Rauf had recognised what had once been his own essential flaw and had tracked it back to its unfortunate source. He had great respect and affection for his mother but she had indoctrinated him with a lot of foolish romantic notions about her own sex that had caused him nothing but grief. But then his naive parent had no concept of the much more basic level at which men and women of Rauf's generation interacted, and regarded his womanising reputation as a source of deep shame.

Whereas Rauf rejoiced in the knowledge that what he had once got wrong, he now always got right. Women passed through his bedroom without causing him any concern that he was taking cruel advantage of their supposedly weaker and more trusting natures. Having shaken off the dangerous misconception that good, old-fashioned lust was love, he enjoyed his male freedom of choice. He would get a kick out of seeing Lily Harris again, he decided. No doubt Lily imagined that her beauty allied with some soppy recollection of their brief relationship might blunt his business acumen and soften his heart towards her: she would soon find out her mistake...

Lily came downstairs lugging her case step by step.

Her three nieces, Penny, Gemma and Joy, were playing in the sitting-room and the sound of their giggles brought a smile to her tense mouth. It said a lot for her older sister, Hilary, that her children were able to laugh like that in the wake of events that might have destroyed a less close-knit family. It was only a year since Hilary's husband, Brett, had walked out to move in with her sister's former best friend.

At the time, Brett and Hilary's youngest daughter, Joy, had been undergoing the last phase of her treatment for leukaemia. Mercifully, Lily's four-year-old niece had since made a full recovery but then, right from the moment Joy's condition had been diagnosed, Hilary had refused to contemplate any other possibility. Lily's sister was a great believer in the power of positive thinking and she had needed every atom of that strength to keep up her spirits in the testing times that had followed.

Lily's father, Douglas Harris, had signed over his comfortable detached house to Hilary and Brett lock, stock and barrel soon after their marriage and had continued to live with them. In the divorce settlement, Brett had been awarded half the value of the marital home, which he had never put a penny into either buying or maintaining, and as a result it had had to be sold. Not long after that development, it had emerged that Lily's father's travel agency, Harris Travel, which Brett had until recently continued to manage, was also in trouble. Just a month ago Douglas Harris, Hilary and her little girls had moved into the tiny terraced house that was now their home for the foreseeable future.

'You should have let me help you with that case!' Hilary scolded from the kitchen doorway. She was a tall, slender woman with short light brown hair, but even her ready smile could not conceal the tiredness of her eyes for she ran herself ragged struggling to keep up her many commitments. 'We have time for a cup of tea before we leave for the airport. Have you said goodbye to Dad yet?'

'Yes, and once we head off he's going to take the girls down to the park—'

'That's great...I was beginning to think we needed a tin-opener to prise him out of that bedroom upstairs!' In spite of her look of relief at the news of that planned outing, Hilary's light-hearted response wobbled a little. 'Once Dad starts taking an interest in life again, he'll be fine. There's no point looking back to what might have been, is there?'

'No,' Lily agreed, averting her gaze from the bright shimmer of tears Hilary was attempting to conceal, for she was well aware that her elder sister held herself responsible for their father having been forced out of the house he had lived in all his life and his subsequent depression. 'Shouldn't we run through my schedule for Turkey again before I leave? My first priority is to see Rauf about—'

'Are you still worrying about that stupid letter his accountant sent?' Hilary gave her a reproachful glance. 'There's no need. As I told you, I've checked the agency books and those payments *were* made. In fact we've kept every part of that agreement and the accounts are in apple-pie order. This business with Rauf Kasabian is a ridiculous storm in a teacup. When he realises that his new accountant has made a gigantic embarrassing mistake, I'm sure he'll be very apologetic.'

Lily's imagination refused to put Rauf in that guise and her thoughts shied away from him again in discomfiture. Hilary always thought the best of people, always assumed that a genuine mistake or simple misunderstanding lay at the foot of problems, she reflected anxiously while her sister poured the tea. Lily, however, was less trusting and more of a worrier. When she had seen that very official letter from Rauf's high-powered accountant she had been shocked by that blunt demand for the return of Rauf's investment, not to mention a request for payments that had already been made.

Indeed, Lily would have been happier if her sister had consulted a solicitor or even another accountant over that demand. However, having seen large sums of money she could ill afford consumed by such professionals during her divorce, Hilary was determined only to request legal or financial advice as an absolute last resort. In addition, Hilary believed that the contract that Rauf Kasabian had signed with their father was watertight. But what if it weren't? What if there *were* a loophole and Rauf just wanted his stake back out of what had proved to be a far from profitable enterprise?

Lily felt very much personally involved. Had she not brought Rauf home to meet her father that investment would never have been made, for at the time Douglas Harris had already dismissed Brett's suggestion that he should borrow from the bank at high rates of interest. Cautious as he had always been in business matters, her father had, however, been tempted by the offer of financial backing from a silent partner that would spread the risk of the ambitious expansion plans his son-in-law had persuaded him into considering.

'Stop worrying about that silly letter,' her sister urged, reading Lily's troubled air with the ease of a woman who had virtually raised her from birth, and then addressing herself to the task of serving out juice and biscuits to her trio of daughters. 'Getting those two villas Brett had built at Dalyan into the hands of a decent estate agent is more of a priority. Once they're sold, the cash-flow problems I'm having at Harris Travel will be at an end. Just make sure a reasonable price is set on them. I can't afford to hang out for the best possible offer.'

'Will do and, if they're looking a bit shabby after lying empty for so long, I'll do what I can with them,' Lily promised, wondering if Hilary was aware that her face still shadowed whenever she mentioned her ex-husband's name, and then feeling horribly guilty that the divorce had been a secret source of intense relief where she herself was concerned.

'The budget would run to a lick of paint but that's about all.' Hilary grimaced, breaking off to settle a sudden squabble between Penny, who was nine, and Gemma, who was eight, both girls carbon copies of their mother with their fine, flyaway brown hair and hazel eyes. 'Aside of that, concentrate on getting in all the sightseeing trips you can and I'll use your feedback to work out some all-inclusive tour packages to Turkey for next spring. I'm determined to take the agency back to its roots. We can't compete with the big travel chains but we *can* offer a personalised exclusive service to up-market travellers.'

'I'll sign up for every tour available.' Lily let her youngest niece Joy climb up onto her knee and hugged her close. She was a little blonde sprite of a child and very slight in build. For endless months she had been weak as a kitten and the sparkling energy that she had regained was a delight to them all.

Leaving the children in the care of their grandfather, Hilary drove Lily to the airport. 'I know you don't want me to say it…but thanks from the bottom of my heart for everything you've done to help out these last few months,' the older woman said abruptly.

'I've done next to nothing and here I am getting a free holiday off you into the bargain!' Lily teased.

'Solo holidays aren't exactly fun and I know that you could've spent the whole summer in Spain if you hadn't turned down that invite from your college friend on our behalf—'

'How did you find out about that?' Lily demanded in surprise.

'Dad heard you on the phone to Maria and, let's face it, I'm sure you're in no hurry to meet that rat, Rauf Kasabian, again.' Hilary sighed with audible regret. 'But there's just no way I can leave the kids and Dad and the travel agency right now.'

Eyes staring dully straight ahead, Lily forced a laugh of disagreement in determined dismissal of her sister's concern. 'This long after the event, I'd be a sorry case if I was still *that* sensitive about Rauf. And don't call him a rat. I mean…what did he do?'

'He was a gorgeous, arrogant louse and he broke your heart!' Hilary countered with an unfamiliar harshness that shook Lily. 'If he wanted female company to wile away his stay in London that summer, he should have picked someone older and wiser. Instead he led you up the garden path and then ditched you without a word of warning.'

At that angry response, Lily turned startled blue eyes to her sister's taut profile. 'I never realised that you felt like that.'

'I hate his guts,' Hilary confided with a shocking lack of hesitation. 'More so since I've realised the damage he did to your confidence. It's unnatural for a girl of your age not to date. You've always been a little shy and reserved but, after what he did, it was like you locked yourself up tight and threw the key away! I'm sorry…I should mind my own business.'

'No, it's all right.' Lily swallowed the aching thickness in her throat, touched by Hilary's loyalty and love but pained by her perception.

Although her sister remained unaware of the reality, she *had* pushed herself out on dates over the past year, hoping to meet someone who might make her feel as Rauf once had and enable her to finally shake free of the past. Only it hadn't happened. But, very fortunately, her sibling had got the actual identity of the man who had most damaged Lily's trust in his sex quite wrong and Lily knew that she would never tell the sister she loved the truth for there would be no gain to be made from causing Hilary such pain now.

Yes, Rauf's sudden defection had hurt her terribly, but then he had never mentioned love or the future and indeed had told her that he had no intention of *ever* getting married. On his terms, what they had shared had only been a minor flirtation. She was not bitter about it. Was it Rauf's fault that she had managed to convince herself that he thought more of her than he in fact had? No, she answered for herself. She had been young, inexperienced and so much in love that she had not wanted to face the unfortunate reality that these days a gorgeous, sophisticated guy expected sex to be part of any relationship, serious *or* casual. Most probably, Rauf had dumped her because she had failed to deliver on that score.

'No, it's not all right,' Hilary muttered unhappily. 'You're almost twenty-four and I really shouldn't be talking to you and interfering in your life as though you're still a teenager.'

An involuntary grin lit Lily's tense face for Hilary was like a mother hen and never stopped interfering. 'Don't worry about it.'

Almost fourteen years older than Lily, Hilary often treated her more like a daughter than a sister. Their mother had died from post-natal complications within days of Lily's birth and from then on Hilary had shouldered a lot of responsibility within their home. Childcare had been arranged for the daylight hours but it had been Hilary who had fed her newborn sister during the night and rocked her to sleep. It had also been Hilary who had sacrificed her chance to go to university sooner than leave her toddler sibling to the charge of an ever-changing series of carers and a father, who had often acted as guide for the tours that had once been the core element of Harris Travel's prosperity.

She was very conscious of how much she owed Hilary, and there was little that Lily would not have done to lighten her sister's current load in life. Between family commitments and the endless challenge of battling to prop up a failing business and live on a shoestring, her sister already had too much on her plate and Lily only wished that she were in a position to do more to help. Unfortunately, during term time, she worked in a nursery school a couple of hundred miles away.

In a few short weeks, when the new school term started,

she would be returning to work and nowhere within reach when Hilary needed an extra pair of hands or even a supportive hug. Unhappily, flying out to Turkey in Hilary's stead was all that lay within Lily's power and, although she dreaded seeing Rauf again, accepting that necessity without dramatising the event felt like the very least she could do in return.

'There's a message for you,' Lily was informed when she finally got to check into her small hotel at two the following morning.

As she trekked after the porter showing her to her room, Lily shook open the folded sheet of paper and then sucked in a sharp sustaining breath.

'Mr Kasabian will meet you at eleven a.m. on the fourth at the Aegean Court Hotel.'

For what remained of the night, she dozed in stretches, wakening several times with a start and the fading memory of vivid dreams that unsettled and embarrassed her. Dreams about Rauf and the summer she had turned twenty-one. Rauf Kasabian, the guy who had convinced her that a woman could actually *die* from unrequited love and longing. How had he done that to her? How had he got past her defences in the first instance? It still bewildered Lily that she, who had until then backed off in helpless distaste from masculine overtures, had somehow felt only the most shocking, soaring happiness and satisfaction when Rauf had been the offender.

When she walked out of her hotel later that morning to climb into a taxi, she felt hot and bothered and so nervous she literally felt sick. The document case she carried contained copies of all the relevant account-book entries and bank statements that Hilary had given her as proof that all dues had been paid over to Rauf's company, MMI, on the correct dates. She was dropped off at an enormous, opulent hotel complex with a long line of international flags flying outside the imposing main doors.

Rauf had not paraded his great wealth in London. In fact she had had no grasp whatsoever of his true standing in the business world until her father had made discreet enquiries through his bank about the male offering him financial backing. Her father's bank manager had suggested that Douglas Harris break out the champagne to celebrate such a generous offer from a business tycoon whom he had described as being one of the richest and most powerful media moguls in Europe.

In the vast reception lounge inside the Aegean Court, Rauf sank back into his comfortable seat, a glass of mineral water cradled between his lean brown fingers for he never touched alcohol during business hours. He was secure in the knowledge that the staff were hovering at a discreet distance to ensure that nobody else sat down anywhere within hearing for it was *his* hotel. Conducting his meeting with Lily in a public area would ensure that formal distance was maintained and keep it brief.

But then he might have staged their encounter in his penthouse apartment on the top floor had it not been for the fact that it was already very much occupied by family members expecting him to join them for lunch. The pushy but lovable trio of matriarchs in the Kasabian family had that very morning elected without invitation to come for a heady spin in his private jet. Rauf suppressed a rueful groan, for his ninety-two-year-old great-grandmother, his seventy-four-year-old grandmother and his mother could in combination be somewhat trying guests. Was it *his* fault that he was an only child and the sole unappreciative focus of their hopes of the next generation?

Shelving that reflection with a wry grimace, he concentrated his thoughts back on Lily. He fully expected, indeed he was even looking forward to, being disappointed when he saw her again. No woman could possibly be as beautiful as he had once believed her to be.

So, it was most ironic that, when Rauf saw the two middle-aged doormen compete in an undignified race to throw the doors wide for the woman entering the hotel, it should be Lily in receipt of that exaggerated male attention that only a very real degree of beauty evoked. Lily, who still seemed to drift rather than walk, her long dress flowing with her fluid movements and baring only slim arms, narrow wrists and slender ankles. As Lily approached the desk, Rauf watched the young clerk rush to greet her and his wide, sensual mouth compressed into a line harder than steel.

Hair the colour of a sunlit cornfield fell all the way to Lily's waist, even longer than it had been that summer. Her modest appearance, though, was pure, calculated provocation, Rauf thought in raw derision. The plain dress only accentuated her classic beauty and anchoring that mane of fabulous golden hair into prim restraint merely imbued most men with a strong desire to see those pale silken strands loose and spread across a pillow.

In fact it was an education for Rauf to watch every man in her vicinity swivel to watch her move past and note how she affected not to notice the stir she caused. But no woman blessed with her perfect features could remain unaware of the gifts she had been born with. Had he not let himself be fooled by that same air of innocence, had he just taken her to his bed and enjoyed her body, he would surely have realised then that she was not only nothing that special, but also a practised little tart.

*   *   *

As Lily headed in the direction that the desk clerk had indicated her heart started to beat very, very fast, indeed so fast that she could hardly catch her breath. She still could not believe that she was about to see Rauf Kasabian again. But then across the wide empty space that separated them she actually saw Rauf rise from his table. Her whole body leapt with almost painful tension and she froze, paralysed to the spot by that first glimpse of him.

He was so very tall. He stood six feet four inches with the wide shoulders, narrow hips and lithe, muscular build of a male in the peak of physical condition. And gorgeous did not *begin* to describe that lean, bronzed face, Lily conceded in dazed acknowledgement. Rauf was so startlingly handsome that even on the crowded streets of London women had noticed him and turned their heads to stare. Lustrous, luxuriant black hair was cropped to his proud head. He had a riveting bone structure overlaid with vibrant skin and tawny eyes that could be dark as bitter chocolate or as pure a gold as the sinking sun.

Her legs behaved like sticks without the ability to bend as she forced herself to move towards him. Her colour was high at the lowering awareness that she had stopped dead to look at him like an impressionable schoolgirl. He did not make the moment easier for her by striding forward to meet her halfway. Instead he stayed where he was, making her come to him. How had she forgotten how he dominated everything around him? How he could entrap her with one mesmerising look from those thick-lashed, brilliant eyes?

Rauf watched her approach. She was a perfect doll, dainty and exquisite as a Meissen ornament. On even that very basic level she had once appealed to every masculine protective instinct he possessed. Rauf drew in a stark short breath. Memory hadn't lied, memory had only dimmed his recollection of her wonderful skin, not to mention those deep blue eyes wide as a child's and fringed by soft brown lashes a baby deer would have envied. The cool intellect that outright rejected the temptation she presented warred with the much more primitive urges of his all-too-male body. When lust triumphed, stirring him into aching sexual tension, Rauf was infuriated by his own weakness.

Lily hovered several feet away, alarmed by the jangling state of her nerves, the terrifying blankness of her mind and the even more demeaning truth that she could not drag her attention from him. 'It's been a long time,' she said breathlessly, almost wincing at the nervous sound of her own voice.

'Yes. Would you like something to drink?'

'Er…pure orange, please.'

Rauf passed on the order to the waiter nearby and turned back to her. 'Let's get down to business, then,' he drawled with intimidating cool. 'I don't have much time to spare.'

CHAPTER TWO

Taken aback by the coldness of that greeting, Lily was grateful for the small hiatus created by the waiter, who stepped forward to swing out a high-backed armchair for her occupation. 'Thank you.'

'My pleasure, *hanim*,' the young man asserted with an admiring smile until a cool word of Turkish uttered by Rauf sent him into hasty retreat.

'You may have noticed that my countrymen go for English blondes in a big way,' Rauf remarked in his dark, deep drawl.

'Yes,' Lily confided ruefully, thinking of the taxi driver who had tried to chat her up and all the discomfiting male attention that she had attracted since her recent arrival.

Yet she was conscious of Rauf's masculine proximity with every fibre of her being and even more aware of the weird tight little knot low in her pelvis of something that felt dangerously like suppressed excitement. Her tension increased for she was as unsettled by her own reactions as she had been at twenty-one, because no other man had ever had that effect on her.

Rauf lifted a broad shoulder in a casual shrug. 'Here, I'm afraid, and in certain other resorts, British female tourists have the reputation of being the easiest to bed in the shortest possible space of time.'

Lily's face flamed. 'I beg your pardon?'

Rauf dealt her a cool golden glance laden with mockery. Being downright offensive was not the norm for him but he was determined to blow her I'm-so-sweet-and-shockable front right out of the water. 'Some Englishwomen go mad for Turkish men, so don't blame the guys for hassling you.'

'I wasn't aware that I was blaming anybody.' Lily's fingers tightened round the document case on her lap. She just could not credit that he was talking to her in such a way and, bewildered by the antagonism she sensed, she allowed her scrutiny to linger on the scornful slant to his beautifully shaped mouth.

Without the slightest warning, she found herself remembering the wicked, unforgettable excitement of those firm, hard male lips on her own. A deep inner quiver slivered through her slight frame and her skin heated. Mortified by the intimate nature of her wandering thoughts, she could not even recall what they had been talking about. Forcing her head up, she encountered intent tawny eyes and stopped breathing altogether.

His lush black lashes dipped to a slumbrous level over his stunning gaze and she shifted on her seat, every muscle tightening, every nerve-ending flaring with agonising immediacy into sensitised awareness. Desperate to break free of the raw magnetic power he exerted over her and shattered that she could still be susceptible to a male who had once rejected her, she tore her eyes from him and muttered with an abruptness that only increased her discomfiture, 'You said that you didn't have much time...so can we discuss this misunderstanding over the contract that you agreed with my father?'

Rauf's shimmering golden scrutiny rested on her evasive gaze with grim amusement and no small amount of satisfaction. So she did want him and that, at least, had not been a total lie like all the rest. He elevated a challenging black brow. 'There *is* no misunderstanding.'

'There *has* to be.' With hands that were betraying a

dismaying tendency to tremble, Lily dug into the document case and dragged out the sheaf of papers that Hilary had put together.

Wondering what on earth she could hope to achieve by going to such pointless lengths in an effort to convince him that his highly qualified investment consultant was incapable of spotting a rip-off when he came across one, Rauf released his breath in an impatient hiss. 'I have no intention of studying those documents. By failing to make the agreed sharing of annual profits your father has been in breach of our contract for more than two years. That's the base line and the only one that counts.'

'Dad would never default on any contract.' Alarm gripping her at Rauf's stubborn refusal even to direct his attention at the papers that she had set on the table, Lily leant forward, frantically swept up the first sheet and extended it herself. 'This is last year's account-book entry. A sizeable sum of money was wire-transferred to an account known as Marmaris Media Incorporated at your Turkish bank in London. I have every identifying detail of that transfer. For goodness' sake, if that's not proof that a major misunderstanding has occurred, what is?'

His interest now fully engaged by what she had said, for he did not use a Turkish bank in London, but making no attempt to accept the proffered document, Rauf gazed at her flushed and anxious face. 'This sounds remarkably like a *misunderstanding* destined to end up in the hands of an international fraud squad.'

Her natural colour draining away, her blue eyes rounding, Lily let the sheet of paper drop back on the pile and gasped, 'What on earth are you trying to suggest?'

'That it seems very suspicious that the trading name Marmaris Media Incorporated should bear such a very close resemblance to the name under which my own companies operate—'

'Which *is* MMI…Marmaris Media Incorporated!' Lily argued in bewilderment.

'No, I rather think that you must know that that is untrue,' Rauf countered with sardonic cool, for he was now convinced that she was attempting to mount some kind of clumsy belated cover-up. 'MMI stands for Marmaris Media International and no part of my holdings trades under any similar name. Any cash paid into an account in the name of Marmaris Media Incorporated has nothing to do with me.'

'Then the money must still *be* there in that wretched account!' Lily exclaimed, immediately believing that she had found out where a fatal error might have occurred in Harris Travel's dealings with Rauf. 'Don't you see? Nobody at Harris Travel realised they'd got the name wrong and the payments have gone into someone else's account…oh, my goodness, suppose they've *spent* it?'

Against his own volition, Rauf was becoming more entertained with every second he spent listening to her spiel. She looked like a live angel and, had he not known what he did know about her, the appeal in her beautiful eyes might have penetrated even his armour-plated cynicism. He lowered his dense black lashes over his appreciative gaze. She ought to be on television creating kiddy-orientated whodunnits of shattering simplicity. That climax of a punchline, 'Suppose they've spent it?' was priceless and he would long cherish its utterance for he had an excellent, if dark, sense of humour.

Nobody with any wit could have been taken in by so unlikely a tale. He was willing to bet a good half of his vast wealth that were he willing to go through the laborious motions she was trying to prompt him into making, willing to act like her trusting ally in pursuit of an unknown criminal, he would find out...guess what? Surprise, surprise, he *didn't* think! The fake account called Marmaris Media Incorporated would be as empty as the old lady's cupboard in the English nursery rhyme. Switching money between accounts to conceal where it was heading next and false entries in the account books were one of the most rudimentary and common methods of concealing fraud.

'Didn't you hear what I said?' Lily prompted, incredulous at his lack of reaction and actually jumping to her feet to stress her enthusiasm for that possible explanation. It seemed obvious that a stupid but simple mistake had sent the payments that Rauf should have received into the wrong bank account. 'Either all those payments have been piling up in one of those dormant accounts that you read about or someone's been having a merry old time for the last two years on money that was rightfully *yours!*'

'Thankfully it's not my problem,' Rauf responded smooth as silk, but he was operating on two levels again, his brain attempting to disengage from his libido as he tensed with growing annoyance. As she automatically angled her slender body towards him he was maddeningly aware of the tantalising thrust of her lush little breasts beneath the shrouding dress and his body hardened on a surge of instant sexual hunger that inflamed his pride.

'But it's your money...don't you care about that?' Deflated and bemused by his apparent disinterest, Lily dared to look at him direct and clashed with smouldering golden eyes.

Her heart skipped a beat and in the interim she felt her full breasts shift inside her cotton bra, the soft tips pinching into sudden taut sensitivity. Rigid with shamed awareness of what was happening to her, she lowered her head and dropped back down into her seat again at speed. Could he still sense the appalling effect he had on her? A crawling sense of humiliation engulfed her, for she had never dreamt that, three years on, she might still be vulnerable around Rauf Kasabian. After all, she wasn't in love with him any more, and he might be a good-looking guy—all right a *very* good-looking guy—but that was no excuse, was it?

Sheer anger having overwhelmed his arousal, Rauf was reminding himself of what a cruel little tease Lily had always been. Once she had drawn him in with the same languishing looks and responsive body language, only to treat him to shrinking reluctance when he had dared to react to those invitations. But her most effective ploy of all had been three quite unforgettable and very clever little words. "You scare me," she had once confided in a breathy little voice of apparent apology, shocking and shaming him into the kind of total physical restraint that he had never had to practise round any other woman.

Still raw from the memory of that unjust and wounding accusation, Rauf squared his wide shoulders, his formidable intelligence now fully back in the ascendant. 'Harris Travel would *still* be in breach of contract and I do wish you luck in pursuing the dormant account scenario. However, all that is owed to me must be repaid—'

Tense as a bowstring, Lily parted dry lips. 'Yes, of course I accept that, but—'

'I don't like being ripped off.' The chill in Rauf's hard dark-as-midnight eyes was now pronounced. 'In fact, with very little encouragement, I can be a total unforgiving bastard.'

'I'm just asking you to be reasonable and examine these papers and you won't even do *that* for me.' Lily regarded him with reproachful blue eyes. 'That's not so much to ask...surely? Why are you treating me like this?'

'Like…what?' Rauf asked in the same cool tone.

'Like we're enemies or something….' Lily muttered uneasily.

'There's nothing deader than a dead love affair, except perhaps an affair that never was,' Rauf spelt out with cutting clarity.

Lily went very still and paled as though she had been struck. She stared with strained intensity at the papers he had refused to scrutinise while she fought to hold back the lowering tears stinging the back of her eyes. There it was, confessed in his own words: the truth of why he had lost all interest in her. *An affair that never was.* It was so belittling to appreciate that what she had believed they'd shared had meant nothing to him without sex. She had always suspected it but that direct confirmation truly hurt. She snatched up her glass of pure orange and took several sips to ease the aching fullness in her throat. Reminding herself that she had much more important matters to concentrate on, she struggled to pull herself back together again.

'Time's running out.' Rauf steeled himself against the artful way she was sitting bolt upright in the chair with the brave but vulnerable aspect of a punished child. As he had already learnt to his cost in the past, she was a very convincing actress and her sole objective then as now had been his wallet, not the wedding ring he had once naively assumed.

Swallowing hard, Lily lifted her head and breathed in deep. 'I'm willing to admit that since we last met, Harris Travel may not have been run quite the way it ought to have been. Two years ago, after a spate of ill health, my father retired and Brett took over. Now he's gone and it's my sister, Hilary, who is managing the business. You say that the contract has been broken and you won't allow any leeway for human error. But if you insist on reclaiming your stake in the agency right now, it may well bankrupt it.'

'Business can be tough. I'm sorry but I'm not prepared to sit through the plucking of a thousand violin strings,' Rauf said very drily, wondering with revulsion where Brett Gilman had 'gone'. The grave? To employment elsewhere? He would not allow himself to ask.

'Brett went off with Hilary's best friend, Janice,' Lily extended heavily and he noted that, just as he recalled from the past, even now when she referred to her sister's husband her eyes were carefully screened in a secretive way. 'Hilary and Brett are divorced now.'

So *that* was why Lily had come all the way out to Turkey to beg his indulgence and bat her fawn-like eyelashes in his direction! Smarmy Brett had scarpered with yet another foolish woman. His lean, strong face taut, Rauf's handsome mouth compressed with distaste. Look beyond the illusory purity of her beauty and Lily was revealed for what she was: an unscrupulous, greedy little schemer, ever ready to tell lies when it suited her to do so. Once, she had been stupid enough to lie to him and in lying had convicted herself with her own tongue.

'I get this feeling that you're really not listening to anything that I say, but what I'm saying is *so* very important,' Lily emphasised in a low intense plea. 'If those payments which you say were never made—'

'I know for a fact that they were never made.' Rafe's aggressive jawline squared. 'Do we have to keep on going over the same ground?'

'Well, if they weren't made, then it was a case of a genuine mistake. Surely you have enough understanding and patience to allow Harris Travel to sort it out?'

'Why should I be patient?' Rauf dealt her an enquiring

glance in which the milk of human kindness was most noticeable by its unapologetic absence. The Turkish builders defrauded by Harris Travel had also practised patience and much good it had done them!

'I don't know you like this...' Lily mumbled sickly, sinking ever deeper into a sense of shock over the extent to which he seemed to have changed. Had Rauf always been so cold, callous and unfeeling? Had she only imagined that she'd seen other finer and more sensitive qualities in him?

She tried afresh to reach him. 'I'm only asking for some more time—'

'No.' Rauf uttered the word in a tone of crushing finality. 'You've wasted enough of my time.'

'Look, I didn't come out here prepared for this awful situation!' Lily protested, her voice rising in spite of her attempt to keep it level, and a flush of embarrassment covered her face as Rauf elevated an ebony brow in meaningful rebuke. 'Couldn't you help me with this? I don't have the resources to check out this bank account mix-up from here.'

Lily down on her knees and begging. Rauf liked the idea even though he knew that he would still pull the plug on the travel agency and cut that last reminder of her out of his life. For his own amusement, would he play along for a little while with her absurd stories and excuses? What would he discover? That she and her family were a set of outright thieves? Reckless thieves too, unable to look ahead and spot the obvious fact that their dishonesty would inevitably be exposed. Then he reminded himself that his own newspapers were full of tales of such foolish fraudsters, who, regardless of the obvious consequences, were quite unable to resist temptation.

Sensing that she finally had his attention, Lily pushed

the documents across the table again. 'Please look these over...and I *can* offer one concrete promise—whatever happens, you will be compensated. Brett built two luxury villas near Dalyan and I have to arrange for them to be sold. Harris Travel does have some assets,' she proclaimed in desperation.

But the biggest asset of all was seated just feet away from him, Rauf conceded, looking direct into her pleading violet-blue eyes, a kind of wonderment laced with cold, deep anger rising at volatile force inside him. He could not credit her gall! How *dared* she feed him such falsehoods? How could she think that he would have agreed to their meeting without having all the facts at his disposal? That Lily should face him with outright lies proved beyond all doubt that she was involved up to her throat in blatant deception! That was the moment that Rauf decided to take a harder line with Lily.

Anxiety holding her taut, Lily noted how very still Rauf had become and her attention lingered on the semi-screened shimmer of his unreadable gaze. Then even as she watched Rauf reached out and swept up the Harris Travel documents he had earlier disdained, sending a surge of hope travelling through her. 'I'm not making any promises,' he asserted in a dark, deep, honeyed drawl that sent the oddest little shiver down her spine.

'Oh, no, of course not...I wouldn't expect that at this point,' Lily hastened to assure him, almost sick with relief at his change of heart and certain that he would be more sympathetic once he had gone over those papers.

'But the amount of time that this tangled affair will consume only comes at a price.' Rauf moved in for the kill, knowing just how much he would revel in making Lily dance to his tune while he kept her in suspense. Hadn't she once done the same to him in a much more primitive way? With raw contempt, he recalled the pseudo-nervous squeaks he had been made to suffer that summer while she had swerved between brief bouts of melting enthusiasm to keep him hooked and sudden attacks of timidity. She had played him like a violin virtuoso, convincing him one hundred per cent that he'd been dealing with a very nervous virgin. But on this occasion, he had the whip hand.

'A…price?' In confusion, Lily frowned, her heart hammering as she noted the gleam of gold in his arresting gaze.

Rauf angled his arrogant dark head back with the measured and confident timing of a hunter about to spring a trap. 'In this world everything comes at a price…haven't you learnt that yet?'

'I'm not sure I follow…' Her oval face taut, a frown marked her smooth brow.

A faint sardonic smile lightened Rauf's lean, dark features. 'It's very simple. If I have to go through these documents in detail, I need your help.'

Her frown evaporating at that statement, Lily sat forward with an air of eagerness, soft blue eyes brightening. 'Certainly…that's not a problem. How could you think it would be?'

'I'm only here in Bodrum for a few hours. Since I have a board meeting in Istanbul tomorrow, I'll be flying back there this evening. Later tomorrow, however, I'm going to my country estate and I suggest that you join me there and stay for a few days,' Rauf murmured levelly. 'It would be more convenient to have you on hand to answer any queries I might have and assist in my inquiries.'

As Rauf delivered that bombshell Lily had parted her lips several times as if she'd been about to speak, but on each occasion caution had made her bite her tongue. She was unnerved by the prospect of staying as a guest in Rauf's country home. However, in the circumstances, his request was a reasonable one. She could hardly expect him to fly back to the coast just for her benefit.

'Yes, all right,' Lily conceded tautly.

Rauf had had no doubt that she would agree and her obvious discomfiture surprised him not at all. Naturally, she could not refuse the opportunity to keep an eye on the course of his inquiries because she would be afraid that he might turn up evidence that would incriminate her and might even be hoping for the chance to bury it again. At the same time, however, she had to continue to play the innocent. Before he took her to Sonngul, he would ensure that they made an unannounced detour to view the 'villas' she had proffered as assets. Even the cleverest liar could not hope to lie her way out of what he intended to confront her with!

'When would you like me to come to your home?' Lily prompted uncomfortably. 'Is it far from here?'

'Quite some distance. I'll make arrangements for you to be picked up at your hotel tomorrow morning at eleven. I'll meet you at the airport, so that we can travel on to Sonngul together.' Studying the soft pink fullness of her lips, Rauf was picturing her splayed like a wanton temptress across his magnificent bed at the old house where he had, out of respect for his family, never taken a woman. Would he...or wouldn't he take advantage of her present eagerness to please? *No*, he decided with fierce determination, he would not. He would take no woman to his bed on such sordid terms.

'Thank you. I appreciate your kindness in making time for this.' Lily felt her lips tingle from his glinting scrutiny and a wave of slow, painful colour warmed her fair complexion. In the pulsing atmosphere, her mouth ran dry and her breathing pattern quickened. She recognised her own excitement, her longing for him to touch her, was shamed by it but not to the degree she had once been when her own contrary physical responses had scared and confused her. But that had not been Rauf's fault or, indeed, even her *own* fault, she conceded with pained regret.

Rauf was offended by that unsought and forbidden image of Lily ornamenting his bed, and his lean, strong face was grim. He could not give credence to the smallest doubt of her guilt now: she had played her part in defrauding him. Once he had assembled the necessary evidence, he would hand her over to the police. He would do what was right and would not be swayed by her desirability or his own lust into compromising either his own ethical code or the honour of the Kasabian family. There should be no distinction between his treatment of Lily and any other wrongdoer. In daring to approach him with her lies and invite his investigation of the facts, she would discover that she had merely precipitated her own punishment and, even worse, had done so in a country with a judicial system far less liberal than that of her own.

That decision etched in stone on his soul, Rauf rose upright, his brilliant dark eyes cool and bright as a mountain spring. 'I'm afraid I must close our meeting here—I have a lunch engagement to keep.'

Disconcerted by that sudden conclusion to their meeting, Lily scrambled up in even greater haste, but by then she had already lost Rauf's attention. Following his frowning gaze, she saw a tiny silver-haired old lady with a stick moving towards them, a helpful young man by her side.

Rauf ground his teeth together as his great-grandmother approached with all the unstoppable determination of a stick-propelled missile. One of the hotel staff must have let drop that his appointment was with a young and beautiful foreigner. That exciting disclosure would have been all it would have taken to shoot Nelispah Kasabian into the penthouse lift and down to the ground floor to satisfy her lively curiosity.

'Mrs Kasabian says...' The hotel executive acting as Nelispah's guide and translator skimmed Rauf a strained glance of apology before turning to address Lily. 'Mrs Kasabian says...what a lovely dress you are wearing!'

Rauf blinked and then scrutinised the billowing folds of Lily's shroud. Yes, he supposed a dress that only hinted that an actual female body existed beneath it was right down his very modest great-grandmother's street. The entire family and their staff conspired to ensure that Nelispah's delicate sensibilities were protected from the shocking moral laxity of a world that would distress her for her heart was weak. Fortunately, she did not watch television or even read the family newspapers because she believed that her late husband would not have approved of her engaging in either activity.

'I have the honour of introducing you to my great-grandmother, Nelispah Kasabian...Lily Harris.' Rauf performed the introduction with gritty reluctance but spoke in soft, gentle Turkish to the little woman, who barely reached his chest in height.

'Please tell her how very happy I am to meet her.' Lily returned Mrs Kasabian's big, beaming smile with warm appreciation.

Resting a frail hand on Rauf's supportive arm, Nelispah chattered on in Turkish while Rauf employed a fast covert signal to send her translator into silenced retreat. 'Lily *hanim* has a sweet smile. I like what I see in this young woman's face,' his great-grandmother confided with alarming enthusiasm. 'Would she like to join us for lunch and tell us about herself and her family?'

Striving not to wince at the threat of what might emerge were Lily to come into contact with the matriarchal interrogation team, Rauf depressed that hope and, with a quiet word of apology to Lily, he walked the old lady back towards the lift. Seeing the affection that had softened his stunning eyes, Lily glanced away again, pained by that contrast to Rauf's abrasive treatment of her.

But then this was a business matter, not a personal one, she reminded herself doggedly. Evidently, Harris Travel had messed up big time when it came to that contract. Had Brett been responsible for that? Although Lily loathed her sister's ex-husband, she knew that both Hilary and her father had been very impressed, not only by the efficient way in which Brett had run the family business, but also by the long hours he had worked. Profits might have sunk to a dismal level but nobody had blamed Brett for that reality. After all, it was hardly his fault that another travel agency had opened up in competition in the same town.

Whatever, Lily was uneasily aware that Rauf had only been willing to relent after she had mentioned the villas that were to be sold. What was going to happen if those payments made into the wrong account could not be tracked down and retrieved? And if the cash from the sale of the villas had to go to Rauf rather than Harris Travel, would Hilary still be able to stay in business? Deciding to wait until she had concrete facts at her disposal before passing on any bad news to her sister, Lily tensed as Rauf returned to her side.

'My limo will take you back to your hotel,' Rauf imparted, shortening his long, fluid stride to her slower pace to walk her outside.

On the pavement, she hovered and stole a strained glance up at him, intimidated and troubled by his continuing detachment. 'This business stuff aside…can't we still be friends?' she heard herself ask in a rush.

As he met her beautiful blue eyes seething derision at

that appeal flamed through Rauf's big, powerful frame, hardening his superb bone structure, firing his fantastic eyes to raw, shimmering gold. It infuriated him that once upon a time he had swallowed her every mushy sentence. 'I'm not five years old and neither are you.'

Lily flushed in embarrassment and cringed for her own impulsive tongue.

'On the other hand, *güzelim*,' Rauf growled soft and low as he reached for her with two lean, purposeful hands and pulled her to him on a surge of anger so strong he did not even question what he was doing, 'I hate to disappoint a woman.'

Pinned into startling connection with six feet four inches of hard, masculine muscle and power, her heart pounding like crazy, Lily gasped, 'Rauf—?'

His wide, sensual mouth came down on hers with explosive force, all the passion of the volatile nature he usually kept in check powering to the surface to drive that kiss. For an instant Lily froze in total shock and then, without any mental prompting she recognised, she stretched up on tiptoe and wrapped her slim arms round his neck. As the first wild wave of response rocked through her trembling length, she loosed a low moan, angling her head back, letting the erotic plunge of his tongue feed from the sweetness of her mouth.

With an abruptness that left Lily in a turmoil of confusion, Rauf set her free again. A dark line of febrile colour scoring his taut cheekbones, he was appalled both by his own reckless disregard of his surroundings and by her unexpected encouragement. Trust Lily to change her game plan when he could least afford her to do so! Such public displays were frowned on by his people. What the hell had come over him?

Her lush mouth reddened from the fiery imprint of his,

Lily focused on Rauf with dazed eyes and a helpless surge of pride in herself. She had stayed in his arms without succumbing to an attack of unreasonable fear. Finally making herself acknowledge those disturbing feelings and openly discuss what had caused them with a counsellor the previous year had worked.

'That will *not* be repeated,' Rauf breathed with icy emphasis, yanking open the door of the long silver limo waiting by the kerb with his own hand. 'There is nothing between us now.'

Then why had he touched her in the first place? Stiff with hurt bewilderment, Lily climbed into the opulent car. She wished she had pushed him away, indeed done anything other than thrown her arms round him in encouragement. She was furious with herself. Here she was almost twenty-four years old, still a virgin and still, it seemed, as immature as an adolescent. Obviously Rauf had reacted to the willing signals that *she* must have been putting out! On the strength of that demeaning conviction, Lily stopped being angry and felt that she had asked to be humiliated.

But then who would ever have forecast that she of all women might ever be guilty of forward behaviour around a male of the species? As Rauf's limousine drove Lily back to her hotel in Gumbet she was pale and taut and already mental miles away from their recent meeting. Memories that she only rarely allowed herself to take out and examine had engulfed her...

Hilary had married Brett when Lily had been only twelve. Delighted to be their bridesmaid, Lily had been thrilled that Hilary had been so much in love and even happier that Brett had been willing to move into their family home rather than take Hilary to live somewhere else. Their father had been equally impressed with Hilary's bridegroom for Brett had always awarded the older man pronounced respect and deference. A year later, Douglas Harris had signed his house over to his daughter and son-in-law.

Just two years after that, when she'd been only fifteen, Lily had had her first sight of Brett with another woman. Heading home from a friend's house, she had cut across a car park on the outskirts of town. Seeing Brett's sports car parked there and the shadow of movement within, she had hurried towards it thinking that she would get a lift with him. Instead she had seen her brother-in-law locked in a passionate embrace with a stranger. Devastated by that sight but grateful that the guilty couple hadn't noticed her, she had been so upset that she had wandered round town for several hours before she'd been able to face going home.

All her life up until that point, Lily had told Hilary virtually everything. But what she had seen that day had deprived her of her only true confidante for she had been painfully conscious that her big sister had worshipped the ground her handsome husband had walked on and had also been heavily pregnant with their second child. Lily had agonised for weeks over what she ought to have done before finally deciding to confide in her father and put the responsibility of that knowledge in his hands.

But in no way had Douglas Harris reacted as his teenage daughter had imagined he might have done. 'You were mistaken,' her father told her in instant angry rebuttal.

'But I saw them…it was Brett and it was his car!' Lily protested.

'Don't you *ever* mention this again and don't you breathe a word of this nonsense to your sister!' the older man censured in even greater fury. 'Brett and Hilary have a very happy marriage. What's got into you that you can make up such a wicked and dangerous story about your own brother-in-law?'

In her turn, Lily was shattered that her usually mild-mannered father could react in such a disbelieving and unjust way to her trusting confession. She had to get older before she could appreciate that her unfortunate parent had too much invested in the stability of Hilary's marriage to easily face the threat that Brett might not be the fine, upstanding young man he had believed him to be. And how could she have foreseen that worry over what she had told him would eventually drive her father to make the very great mistake of warning Brett that he had been seen in that car park?

Faster than the speed of light, for there was nothing slow about Brett's survival instincts, Brett added two and two together and worked out *who* had seen him. That same afternoon he picked Lily up from school and frightened the living daylights out of her with his rage and his threats. Then and there Lily's happy home life and her faith in the adults around her came to a harsh and final end.

'You sneaky little bitch!' Brett roared at her, after shooting his car into the *same* car park in an act of intimidation that she soon learned was pure Brett Gilman. 'From here on in, you'd better mind your own bloody business. Haven't you ever heard of the three wise monkeys? Speak no evil, hear no evil and see no evil. Tell tales on me again and you won't *have* a home any more…I'll tell Hilary that her precocious little sister has been trying it on with me and she'll believe me long before she'll believe you!'

Lily then learnt what it was to live in fear. Resenting her, and determined to punish her for exposing his womanising ways to Douglas Harris, Brett gloried in his power over Lily and soon worked out the kind of treatment that would make her feel most threatened. Out of her sister's sight and hearing, he began to look at Lily's developing curves in a way that made her skin crawl and taunt her with crude familiar comments. He never actually touched her but she lived in terror that some day he *might*.

By the time Lily escaped her home to start her teacher-training course at a college a long way away, Brett had turned Lily into a silent, secretive and timid teenager, who covered every possible inch of her body and who went in genuine fear of male aggression and sexuality.

Surfacing from her recollections of that traumatic period of her life, Lily found a sheen of perspiration on her skin. When she went for a shower in her room, she reminded herself that that nightmare was in the past. Yet her most bitter regret was still that the damage Brett had inflicted had almost inevitably destroyed any hope of her having a normal relationship with Rauf Kasabian when she had first met him.

Three years on, Rauf was hostile, cold and detached in a way that Lily had never dreamt he could be and she was much too vulnerable. Lily recognised with shamed self-honesty that she would still do just about anything to get a second chance with Rauf. But he had made it clear that he had no intention of getting involved with her again.

Could she even blame him for that? Lily asked herself as she lay in bed that night. If anything, Rauf had been kind when he'd described what they had had as the affair that never was. With pained hindsight, Lily knew that Rauf might have utilised more hurtful candour. He might have told her that blowing hot and cold with a man was a huge turn-off and that treating a decent guy like a ravenous sex beast was an even less enthralling experience...

CHAPTER THREE

THE summer after she finished her second year at college, Lily had taken a temporary job working as a waitress in a fashionable London bar while she looked for a suitable position as a nursery nurse.

Within the first week, Lily had begun dreading going into work for she hadn't been able to easily handle the sort of teasing and touching that the other waitresses had withstood from the male customers. However, her salary plus the generous tips she'd received had met the rent on the tiny apartment she'd been sharing and had made it possible for her to avoid having to return home and live under the same roof as Brett.

Rauf had come in with a female in tow one lunchtime.

'Why are all the *really* gorgeous men already spoken for?' Annabel, her flatmate since first year and fellow waitress, lamented while she and Lily waited at the counter for their orders.

'Who have you noticed now?' Lily groaned, accustomed to Annabel's frequent complaints about the extreme rarity of the free and fanciable male.

'He's sitting down with the brunette in the sexy white dress.'

Lily glanced over. His commanding height and build, the slashing angle of his high cheekbones, strong nose and wide, passionate male mouth combined with his lustrous black hair made him stand out from the common herd all right. But she would have looked away again had not Rauf thrown his arrogant dark head back as he sat down and let her see his extraordinary eyes. Tawny gold as polished tiger's-eye stones reflecting the light, riveting, beautiful, utterly hypnotic. Involuntarily she stared, heartbeat kicking up pace, breathing fractured, her whole body tight and tense as if she was waiting for something indescribably exciting to happen. Then his narrowed gaze clashed with hers and it was as if somebody had switched on Christmas lights inside her. Suddenly she was electric, wired, alive for the very first time.

'And wouldn't you just know it?' Annabel muttered resentfully as she watched Rauf appraise Lily's glowing blonde beauty with predictable male intensity. 'I might as well be invisible but he's *yours* for the asking. You should wear a little "I'm gay" badge, Lily…at least it would stop the guys wasting their time and let the rest of us get a look-in!'

Aghast at the startling content of that disgruntled little speech, Lily shot her attention back to Annabel. 'Say that again?'

Annabel just shrugged. 'Well, you *are*, aren't you? You might still be in the closet but the way you feel about men makes it pretty obvious. I guessed ages ago.'

'I'm *not* gay…' Lily countered in whispered but emphatic denial as Annabel lifted her laden tray.

'Look, it's none of my business.' Annabel grimaced. 'I was only being a jealous cow about your looks.'

Shaken that someone she had known for two years could have got her so wrong, Lily went to serve Rauf. Not once did she look directly at him or his companion but, even in the ennervated state she was in, she noted his rich, dark drawl and the faint exotic accent that edged his excellent English. Disaster only struck when she delivered their drinks. As she tried to set the glass of red wine down the brunette made a sudden snatch at it mid-air and their hands collided. The glass fell, spilling a cascade of ruby-red liquid down onto the woman's lap.

'You stupid girl!' the irate brunette screeched, behaving as though she had been subjected to a deliberate assault. 'Wasn't coming on to my man enough for you? Did you have to ruin my dress too?'

As Lily's boss hurried to the scene and Lily proffered napkins and apologies that were ignored while really wanting to sink through the floor in chagrin, Rauf dropped a banknote on the table and herded his hysterical lunch date out at speed. Lily didn't expect ever to see him again. But the next day when she turned up for her shift a beautiful bouquet was waiting for her along with a card.

'Sorry that you were embarrassed yesterday. Rauf'

'When a bloke spends about a hundred quid on flowers, it certainly tells me *who* was coming on to *who*,' her female boss quipped with considerable amusement.

Emerging from the powerful pull of the past, Lily needed enormous effort to shut down the surging tide of memory keeping her awake. What did it say about her that she should still be so obsessed with a relationship that Rauf had long since left behind him? Angry at her lack of self-discipline, Lily told herself to grow up.

The next morning, Rauf flew in on a sleek private jet half an hour after Lily arrived at the airport. In the brilliant sunlight of midday, she watched him emerge and descend the steps with the fluid, measured pace of a very self-assured male. Sheathed in a beautifully tailored dove-grey business suit, he looked stunningly handsome and, even at a distance, his bold bronzed features emanated all the decisive authority of his forceful personality. Exchanging a laughing word with the official waiting to greet him, he paused, lean, strong face settling back into striking gravity again as he aimed a cool-eyed glance at Lily where she waited just inside the building.

'You can go through now, Miss Harris,' she was told.

Rauf watched her walk towards him. Clad in a pale blue dress and a cardigan that had to be roasting her alive in the heat of midsummer, golden hair glittering in the bright light, Lily looked apprehensive and very young.

An insane impulse to urge her to turn back and board the first available flight home assailed Rauf. Faint colour demarcating his hard cheekbones, his jawline clenched hard. Had she been a man, he would have harboured no second thoughts. So who was being sexist? He was only doing to her what she had once done to him: luring her down a path that would look safe until the very last moment. How would she react when she found herself staring into the abyss with the police waiting to make an arrest on the other side?

As yet, he hadn't called in the police, hadn't identified her to them. But the gendarme in the village where the villa project had misfired already had a file prepared on the case. Furthermore, Lily, Rauf had discovered, was now listed as a director of Harris Travel on the firm notepaper and as such could be held liable. But what Rauf wanted most of all was Brett Gilman's head on a plate.

'It's hot,' Lily murmured as she drew level with him.

'And likely to get hotter,' Rauf imparted in his distinctive drawl, a light hand touching her spine just enough to turn her in the direction of the helicopter sitting parked.

'Will it be a long flight?'

'About an hour or so in all. We're making a stop on the way.' Without hesitation, Rauf made a smooth change of subject. 'How are you enjoying your stay so far?'

'I'm still getting acclimatised. Next week, I'm going to sign up for all the trips and see the sights. Hilary's hoping to organise special tours for the spring...' Lily said, her voice petering out as Rauf closed his hands round her waist and lifted her up into the helicopter as if she weighed no more than a child. 'Thanks.'

As he settled in beside her and signalled the pilot, the rotor blades began to whir. Lily struggled to tighten the seat belt, which had been loosened to hold a much larger frame than her own. Rauf leant over to assist and she tensed, soft brown lashes flying up on uncertain blue eyes to connect with reflective gold. Her hands fell from the clasp and let his take over. As he bent his dark head his luxuriant black hair brushed her chin. Breathing in the warm, achingly familiar scent of him, she trembled, feeling her breasts lift and stir beneath her dress and the tender tips swell into prominence, and biting her soft lower lip in an agony of discomfiture.

She wanted to plunge her fingers into his silky black hair and drag his mouth up to hers again and she was shocked rigid by the depth of her own longing. In the midst of such crazy promptings, she didn't know herself. What was it about him that he could reduce her to such a level without even trying? Mouth bone-dry, her fingers curled in on themselves lest they too developed a will of their own, she only breathed again when he had settled back into his own seat.

For the entire flight, she stared out the window. She had a fantastic view of the bright turquoise sea studded with islands and edged by tall crags and sandy beaches before the helicopter went into a turn and headed inland. When the coastal development was left behind, she saw the ruin of a castle built on bare rock, hazy tracts of soft green pine forest, the occasional dust road leading out miles through tiny cultivated fields and orchards to small clusters of re-mote dwellings. She remembered Rauf telling her that virtually every family had links with a village and would often maintain contact with their roots there generations after they had taken up residence in a town.

After the tranquil, soothing scenes of beautiful unspoilt countryside, it was something of a surprise to Lily to see a coalmine come into view as the helicopter started to land. Coalmining was a business, she reminded herself, and Rauf *had* mentioned a stop on the way. Perhaps one of his newspapers or magazines was doing a feature on the mine, she thought dimly.

Springing out of the craft, Rauf swung back to extend a hand to her. Lily stepped out onto waste ground and saw a dust road several yards ahead of them.

Level dark golden eyes zeroed in on her. 'Do you know where you are?'

Lily shook her golden head and wondered how on earth he could imagine she would know. 'I haven't a clue.'

'I think you'll solve the mystery soon enough,' Rauf asserted, leading her across the road towards a steep paved driveway edged with fancy carriage lamps and really the very last kind of opulent entrance one would have expected to see within yards of the fencing that surrounded the mine.

Lily frowned. 'Is this where you live?'

'Even the locals don't live in this neck of the woods. Who wants to look out the windows and see the slag-heaps?' Rauf derided.

Some sixth sense she had finally picked up on the scorn that edged his every sentence, the strange challenge in his watchful gaze. A wave of tension infiltrated her. She stared back at him, her slender body very taut. He withstood that appraisal with unflinching assurance and her cheeks warmed with self-conscious colour, for he might look intimidating in his current mood but he also looked drop-dead gorgeous. Unhappily that reality kept on playing havoc with her concentration.

'So if you don't live here, where are we going?' Lily prompted, dry-mouthed.

'I decided to surprise you with a flying visit to the villas built by Harris Travel,' Rauf responded drily.

Lily blinked and then a startled laugh fell from her lips. 'Then I'm afraid you've got the address wrong. The villas are near Dalyan, which I understand is quite a beauty spot.'

As she came to a halt Rauf closed a hand over hers. Disconcerted by that move, she flexed her fingers in his and then stilled as a sensation of warmth travelled up her arm, making her outrageously aware of him. He drew her on up the long, winding driveway and then came to a halt, releasing her fingers at the same moment. 'This is the land Brett Gilman bought for a song because nobody else wanted it.'

Closing both of her hands together in front of her, Lily stared at him. 'It can't be…for goodness' sake, this doesn't even look like a tourist area. I'm telling you this is definitely *not* where our villas were built—'

'Since it was my money that financed the project, do you honestly believe I could make such a mistake?'

Lily sucked in a slow, steadying breath of the hot still air and struggled to think straight. 'You were only a silent partner—'

'That was my mistake. Had I insisted on tighter control and greater input, what Harris Travel did here would not have happened because I would not have *allowed* it to happen,' Rauf spelt out with fulminating emphasis.

'What do you mean by…"what Harris Travel *did here*"?' Lily questioned uneasily, her tension mounting with every second that passed. 'Why aren't you listening to me? This isn't where the villas were built.'

'Stop feeding me that bull!' Rauf ground out with raw impatience, lean, powerful face taut and unyielding. 'I have a copy of the contract that Brett signed with the builders in my pocket and a copy of the land purchase deed as well.'

'I don't care if you've got your entire filing cabinet in your pocket!' Lily slung back an entire octave higher, her temper flaring without warning because nothing he had said or done since the helicopter had landed had made sense to her. 'I have photographs of the villas when they were almost complete and the view from the front of the villas was fantastic…there was no wretched coalmine in it!'

'You couldn't possibly have photographs.' Rauf subjected her to a raking appraisal, furious at her stubborn refusal to stop lying even in the face of the overwhelming evidence confronting her.

The driveway had petered out on the brow of the hill, Lily noted somewhat belatedly. A driveway that led to nowhere and nothing? In the act of fumbling in her bag for the wallet of photos that Hilary had told her Brett had brought back from his final visit to Turkey the previous winter, Lily stilled in momentary bewilderment to scan the empty, overgrown ground surrounding her on all sides.

Suddenly Lily laughed, relief coiling through her. 'There are no villas here even to make a mistake *about*! Why won't you just admit that we're in the wrong place?'

While Rauf continued to watch her much as though she had made a sudden claim that she could fly without wings, Lily walked over to him with some satisfaction to extend the photos. 'Our villas, Rauf.'

In seething frustration, Rauf gave the half dozen snaps a cursory appraisal. 'Which proves *what*, Lily? That someone with a camera can take pretty pictures of someone else's building site? Now either you start telling the truth or I let the police handle this investigation.'

Freezing where she stood at that threat, Lily gazed back at him wide-eyed. 'The...*police*?'

'Harris Travel ripped off the local builders and suppliers. The builders were given a fake name and address for the firm and a fake phone number.'

Pale as she stood there under the relentless sun, a trickle of nervous perspiration running down between her breasts, Lily parted her soft lips, but it was a second or two before her voice picked up sufficient strength to emerge. 'Harris Travel ripped off people? I...I don't know what you're talking about.'

Rauf expelled his breath in an impatient hiss. 'There *are* no villas. Nothing was ever built beyond that entrance and you have to know that.'

Lily gulped. Only then did she recall him saying that he had a copy of the land purchase agreement. Surely that was indisputable proof that she was standing on the site that Brett had bought? But this was not the land that Brett had photographed and there were no buildings within view.

'Are you sure the villas aren't just down the road?' she mumbled, peering round herself with frowning incomprehension. 'I want to see that purchase agreement.'

Rauf extended it and Lily grabbed at it. The document trembled along with her hand. It was written in Turkish but when she scanned down the sheet she recognised Brett's signature and an official seal. Her brain was now functioning in very slow motion. Shock was setting in hard and she could not accept the enormity of what Rauf was telling her. 'I still think these villas have got to be around here somewhere...if we look. I mean, maybe we're on the wrong road or something,' she suggested shakily. 'You were always telling me how vast this country is…you can't know *every* road around here!'

She was shaking like a leaf in a high wind. But Rauf was determined not to fall victim to what innate cynicism warned was most likely to be a performance aimed at convincing him that she was a misunderstood innocent. At the same time, however, he could not help but be impressed by the rendering of stupefied shock and disbelief that Lily was giving him.

'There are no villas,' he said again.

'There's *got* to be!' Lily launched at him in feverish protest.

'The land was bought, the builders engaged,' Rauf advanced in a grim undertone. 'But after a small first-stage payment was received, they neither heard from your sister's ex-husband again, nor were they able to establish contact with him.'

Lily tottered backwards and sank down on a low rock in the shade of a spreading chestnut tree. Her legs felt all wobbly and hollow.

'Before the builders discovered that they had been had, they put in the driveway and the foundations. Since the mine shut down, there isn't much employment round here and the builders were promised bonuses for fast results. Gilman had a big car and they thought he was rich, so they went ahead and bought more supplies on credit with a relative, trusting that the next, much larger payment was in the pipeline. Two families were plunged into poverty and debt by this.'

Lily's tummy gave a sick lurch, shame enveloping her. What had happened? What had Brett done? Could he have used the cash earmarked for the villas just to keep the agency in business? She hated Brett, could not initially comprehend her own reluctance to accept the obvious until she acknowledged that the security of her entire family rested in that same balance.

Evidently, Brett had lied over and over again about the villas. He had shown Hilary and their father photographs of another site and had later given them more pictures of that same site and the two big villas that had been erected there. Neither her sister nor her father could have had any suspicion that there was anything suspect about the enterprise because that building project had been Brett's baby from the outset. By then, her father had retired and Hilary had only gone back to work in Harris Travel after Brett had stepped down from managing it just a few months ago...until then, Brett had had an entirely free hand.

So what had happened to all the money that should have gone into building the villas? Brett could only have taken all those thousands of pounds for himself. There were no villas, just a piece of scrubby land with no outlook in the back end of nowhere. Yet Brett had contrived to argue during his divorce settlement with her sister that he was entitled to half of the marital home because Harris Travel would be retaining the sizeable asset of two luxury villas abroad. In addition, Brett had managed to satisfy an admittedly unsuspicious pair of solicitors that those two villas *did* exist. Her poor sister had ended up being grateful that her estranged husband had not also claimed a right to a share of the family firm after all his years working there!

Lily stared into space with shattered eyes. *There were no villas.* That meant that Rauf's investment had gone missing altogether. What chance now was there that that supposed mix-up over those bank account names was genuine? She shuddered and, lifting nerveless hands, she pressed them to her clammy face. Brett had been embezzling from the business and, by the looks of it, he had sucked Harris Travel dry. Her family was going to be left penniless and in debt.

Rauf studied Lily, who was seated like a traumatised pixie on her rock, transfixed by shock. She kept on looking at the overgrown foundations as if she were still hoping that two villas would spring into literal being right there before her very eyes.

'I can't credit this…' she muttered, shaking her head. 'How could Brett do this to his own family? I mean, they've already lost so much since the divorce.'

Smouldering dark golden eyes pinned to her ashen face as she uttered that first-ever disparaging comment on Brett Gilman, Rauf growled, 'You had no idea?'

Blinking, Lily lifted her golden head and looked at him for the first time in several minutes, blue eyes stricken pools as she endeavoured to come to terms with the sheer scale of Brett's lies. 'How can you ask me that? One of the main reasons I'm here in Turkey was to *sell* those villas! I can hardly get my mind round the concept that they were never built in the first place…'

'That's understandable.' So, on the count of the non-existent villas at least, he had misjudged her, Rauf conceded grudgingly, his wide, taut shoulders squaring below the fine, expensive cloth of his jacket. It seemed that Brett Gilman, regardless of his former liaison with Lily, had acted alone and without her knowledge. That would be a shock for her too though: the wounding discovery that her one-time secret lover had lied to her as well, while he'd plunged the family business into fraudulent dealings. But then over the past year, Lily had already suffered a certain amount of punishment, he reminded himself grimly. Brett choosing to divorce her sister for a woman other than herself must have been quite a slap in the face too. But a very well-deserved slap, Rauf reflected without hesitation.

The thick fullness of tears in her throat, Lily compressed her tremulous lips. 'But you *knew*, didn't you? You knew there were no villas when we met up yesterday.'

'I only learned of this scandalous affair forty-eight hours ago when my investment consultant finally brought it to my attention. As I too have a stake in Harris Travel, I have already instructed that the two Turkish families who sustained losses through this venture are to be fully compensated.'

Lily stared at him through swimming eyes. He was so detached from her, so controlled. A helpless sob bubbled in her throat. 'That's good,' she said in a wobbly voice. 'But I doubt very much that you're about to compensate *my* family for their losses!'

Striding forward, Rauf bent down to curve his lean hands round her shaking shoulders and raise her upright. 'Let's get out of here.'

'I feel so awful…like it's somehow my fault!' Lily sobbed, her distress taking her over for a couple of seconds before she contrived to get a grip on herself again. 'But I've never had anything much to do with the business and I still can't understand how Brett could literally steal from his own kids. Goodness knows, I hate him, but Hilary and Dad always had a *very* high opinion of his business acumen!'

Rauf smiled a not very nice smile above her down-bent golden head and closed a supportive arm round her slender back. Her tears would not soften him. Having cracked her façade, he had her on the run and he would keep up the pressure until he knew everything there was to know. He supposed a lot of women would embrace a selective memory when it came to an indefensible affair that should never have happened, but he felt that she owed him, at least, the truth. 'You didn't always *hate* your brother-in-law—'

'Not when he and Hilary first married—'

'And *not* when you brought me home to invest in the family firm at Brett's instigation either,' Rauf slotted in with harsh clarity.

'Sorry?' Lily whipped round to throw him a startled glance. Brett's instigation? How had he known that Brett *had* played a part in her decision to finally take Rauf home to meet her family? But what Rauf said next soon wiped that seeming irrelevancy back out of her mind again.

'Do you think I didn't eventually work out that that was a set-up?' Rauf dealt her contemptuous appraisal from shimmering golden eyes. 'Harris Travel needed an investor and I was rich. Are you trying to say that it was pure coincidence that you decided to introduce me to your family at that particular time? I don't think so!'

'Is that what you believed?' Lily was appalled at that accusation coming out of nowhere at her. How could he have thought that she could be that mercenary and calculating?

'Despite what you seem to think, I didn't come down in the last shower of rain,' Rauf derided, utilising the colloquial speech he had acquired attending an English public school.

'Back then I had no idea how wealthy you were!' Lily slung at him in angry reproach. 'Nor did I find out about the expansion plans for the business until after we arrived that weekend and we both heard Brett and Dad talking. The only reason I took you home was because my sister was dying to meet you!'

'I wish I could believe you,' Rauf breathed in a fierce undertone.

'So you decided that I had been after your money all

along…' Lily framed shakily, stinging tears burning in her darkened eyes. 'And how do you justify believing that when that same weekend I took you aside and suggested you think very carefully before you invested in Harris Travel? And what did you tell me? "This is business, Lily, not something you know much about"!'

Thrown by that unsettling reminder, Rauf opened his mouth to point out that her apparent lack of self-interest might also have been a very effective means of spurring him on to demonstrate his generosity towards her family. But in the end, he said nothing. After all, he was seeing a side of Lily that she had never allowed him to see before and he had no desire to silence her. There she was, practically jumping up and down with rage in front of him, the ultra-feminine, vulnerable front nowhere to be seen, and he was fascinated by that sight.

'You knew it *all*, didn't you?' Lily accused in her furious turmoil, little pearly teeth visibly gritted. 'But now it's all gone wrong, you're blaming me! Well, I'm sorry, but the only mistake I ever made with you, the only thing I have to regret, is that I was ever *stupid* enough to fall in love with you!'

Brushing past him on that final ringing assurance, Lily sped back across the dust road and fairly leapt into the helicopter, no assistance required. She turned her head away when Rauf boarded. She was convinced that she would never look him in the face again after losing control to the extent of admitting that she had been in love with him that summer. How could she have lowered herself to that level? He hadn't been entitled to that ego-boosting confession.

The helicopter lifted into the air. Rauf snatched in a slow, steadying breath. No way could he have got everything so wrong. He was too clever to have misread the evidence. But maybe Lily's tacky affair with Gilman had been on the wane by the time he himself had entered her life, maybe it had even been over...yeah, sure, she had been slinking shiftily out of that hotel with Gilman that afternoon for entirely innocent reasons and had lied about where she had been for entirely innocent reasons too? That was about as likely a possibility as her being the virgin she had sworn she was at the time!

His lean, devastating features set into aggressive lines. He was furious with himself. He was letting her get to him and work her wiles on him again. All she had had to do was tell him she had been in love with him and he had started doubting his own intelligence! But not for nothing had Rauf's own mother deemed her son to be as stubborn in his convictions as a steel-wrapped rock set in concrete. Rauf knew exactly why Lily was tempting him again. His hormones had no discrimination and her draw was pure sex. Even in that prim cardigan, she sent his temperature rocketing!

But then Lily still had that pulling power only because she was incredibly beautiful and he had never been her lover. While she had been screaming at him through gritted teeth, he had been watching the sun gild her glorious hair, noting the delectable prominence of her breasts when she threw her slim shoulders back and wondering if she would unleash that same passion in his bed. Shifting in an effort to ease the tormenting ache of his lingering arousal, Rauf veiled reflective dark golden eyes. Why shouldn't he find out?

After all, it was pretty obvious that if she was innocent of all blame when it came to the villas that never were, she was hardly likely to be involved in the accounts scam either. Gilman had moved on and doubtless taken his ill-gotten gains with him and Rauf would track him down and hang him high with pleasure for his sins...

CHAPTER FOUR

WITH pointed deliberation, Lily ignored Rauf's proffered hand when the helicopter landed for the second time and stepped out alone.

Lily wouldn't look at Rauf either, felt she couldn't trust herself that far. That unfamiliar rage had emptied her, shaking her to her very depths with its ferocity. Yet after the revelations that Rauf had dropped on her without warning, she was only reeling into a state of deeper shock.

'Where are we?' she asked, focusing on his blue silk tie, and her mind in such conflict that she was thinking half a dozen other thoughts all at once. That he had decided she was a gold-digger without any justification. That, with even less reason, he had been prepared to believe she and presumably her entire family had conspired to defraud him along with Brett. That he had with a cool deliberation that chilled her to the marrow flown her out to that abandoned building site to confront her with Brett's crooked dealings. That he also seemed to believe not a single word that she said.

Therefore she didn't need to ask, indeed she already knew without being told that Rauf Kasabian had not the tiniest shred of sympathy for her or her sister or her sister's children or her father.

'Sonngul, my country estate...and I don't know about you,' Rauf imparted, 'but I could do with a drink.'

A slight tremor ran through Lily's whip-taut frame. She was terrified of breaking down in tears. She knew that that was the natural outcome of shock but she didn't want to let herself down in front of him. In every way that mattered, Rauf seemed to be the enemy and a very ruthless one too. He would set the police on Brett and, although Lily would have loved to see Brett banged up in a prison cell, she could only shudder at the prospect of what that same reality would mean to Hilary and her daughters.

Her family lived in a small town and people were never kind when it came to fraud or bankruptcy. Hilary might be divorced from Brett but Harris Travel was still their father's business and that was what people would remember longest. Having been betrayed by her husband and lost her former home into the bargain, Hilary would now have to face not only the scandal and shame of Brett's prosecution, but also the loss of her family's only means of support. It would break Lily's father too, for the sole source of pride the older man still possessed was his good name. They would all be lambs to the slaughter.

As Lily accompanied Rauf down a path screened in and shaded by a wealth of lush overhanging foliage she broke the silence. 'I must phone Hilary. She needs to be told about the villas.'

'I can't agree to you informing your sister at this point. In fact I don't want you communicating with anyone back in England.'

Glancing up in astonishment at that forbidding assurance, Lily met the unashamed challenge in Rauf's steady gaze.

'Your sister may be divorced from Gilman but I doubt that she could be trusted to keep so much bad news to herself. She's much more likely to demand an explanation from Gilman and I don't want him to realise that he's been found out until all the facts have been established,' Rauf explained.

Lily snatched in a sustaining breath. 'What *you* want may not be what I think best for my family!'

'But if you want me to ease your family's passage through this, you'll do as I ask. If you choose to go up against me, remember that you were warned.' Golden eyes hard as a polished wall rested on her shaken face.

'You're threatening me,' Lily whispered sickly.

'No, I'm not,' Rauf contradicted with cool conviction. 'I'm just pointing out the facts. At this moment, I have no reason to trust your sister or your father but I'm willing to withhold judgement in the short term. However, if one of you were to tip off Gilman, accidentally or otherwise, he might disappear and I would then have good cause to wonder whether or not he really was the *only* thief in your family.'

'Thanks a bundle...' Lily muttered, flags of chagrined colour blooming across her taut cheekbones as she absorbed that telling speech.

'You need to know where you stand.'

Between his foot and the ground and in danger of being crushed. Oh, yes, she understood the message she was receiving. Either she left her sister in ignorance or she invited Rauf to suspect either Hilary or their father of having been in league with Brett. 'Am I your hostage now?' Lily demanded.

Rauf paused and from below dense black lashes cast her a molten-gold glance that was as erotic as a caress. 'Would you like to be?' he asked huskily.

That easily he churned up the atmosphere between them. She was disconcerted and trapped by those stunning eyes of his, and a tiny flame of awareness lit low in Lily's tummy; it happened so fast it left her breathless. Tearing her gaze in dismay from his, she focused in a daze on the extraordinary house that had come into view. It sat like a fantasy painting surrounded by venerable oak trees and Lily just stared. With a domed roof and an overhanging first floor, it had all the appearance of a medieval building for, unless she was very much mistaken, it also seemed to be made entirely of wood.

'Sonngul,' Rauf said with perceptible pride. 'The Kasabian *yali*…that means summer home. I had it restored two years ago as a surprise for my great-grandmother.'

A summer home the size of a mansion. Lily breathed in deep.

'Of course, I also built a large extension at the rear,' Rauf continued. 'In the original house, cooking and washing were done in the courtyard. There were no bedrooms either. The family slept in the same areas where they lived by day.'

The arched front door stood wide. It was an airy house of open spaces, tall windows with shutters, soaring ceilings, plays of filtered light and shadow. At the entrance he removed his shoes and a second later she followed suit. Up the sweeping carved staircase on the first floor was a huge room with doorways leading off in several directions and Rauf told her that it was called the *basoda*. Each corner of the room was a distinct and different area, one furnished for dining, another with bookshelves and a desk. Rauf strode up the single shallow step into the furthest corner and opened a drinks cabinet. There opulent cushioned divans edged the walls and created a charming window-seat into the tall bay that overlooked a tranquil river and the dense woods beyond. Slipping off her cardigan, Lily sat down there, soothed by that beauty and the silence.

Unasked, Rauf brought her a brandy. Lily sipped and grimaced, for she had never liked the taste of alcohol, but the fiery spirit helped to disperse the chilled knot of apprehension still keeping all her muscles taut.

Rauf set his own glass down untouched and studied her with level dark golden eyes. 'I misjudged you yesterday,' he murmured with wry honesty. 'I was also very rude. That is unlike me but the whole time that I was with you, I was angry and I wanted to hurt you.'

Surprised by his candour, Lily nodded jerkily, compressed her lips and then dropped her head because the over-emotional tears were threatening her again. Finally she was getting a glimpse of the male she had once fallen hopelessly in love with. A guy who was incredibly proud and very stubborn but who would acknowledge when he was in the wrong even though it killed him to own up to being anything less than perfect. A passionate and very masculine male, who could be domineering and arrogant but who had still been capable of melting her heart with one rueful charismatic smile. But then mercifully, she thought crazily as she fought the moisture dammed up behind her aching eyes, Rauf had *not* smiled since her arrival in Turkey.

'Why would you want to hurt me?' she muttered unevenly, for she could think of no good reason in the world why he should have experienced such a need. He had been the one to walk out of her life. He had not looked back either, but it had been a very long time before she had answered the phone in her student flat without a prayer in her heart that it would be him calling her. But then wasn't she forgetting his current suspicions about her, or at least her family, having been involved in Brett's dishonesty? She shut out that unwelcome recollection for, as matters stood, she had neither control nor influence over the events that would enfold.

Rauf vented a roughened laugh. 'How can you ask me that?'

Lily looked at him, recognised the raw tension in that

lean, strong face that had once haunted her dreams and her heart skipped a beat.

'You must *feel* the hunger you rouse in me,' Rauf breathed with driven emphasis. 'I neither expected that nor sought its return, but that desire for you is still there inside me just as it was that summer.'

Through the open sash-window behind her, Lily could hear the soft rushing sound of the river flowing and rippling over stones and, in the silence that fell, it seemed to fill her eardrums while she tried to absorb what he had just admitted. Was he saying that he wanted her back? Why else would he admit to still desiring her? Slowly, she lifted her head high, faint pink chasing the pallor from her lovely face, astonished blue eyes finally connecting with his fierce measuring appraisal.

'Do you always want most what you think you can't have?' Lily whispered shakily.

'*Evet*…yes,' Rauf admitted in Turkish with a fatalistic shrug as if that state of affairs went without saying as the norm for him.

'So I say no and get wanted even more…you shouldn't have told me that,' Lily tried to tease, wanting to laugh and cry at the same time, and then the tears pounced when her guard was down and streamed in rivulets down her cheeks, startling her as much as they seemed to startle him.

'Lily…*no*…' After an instant of hesitation, Rauf found himself sinking down by her side to draw her into his arms, only to still the motion when she was mere inches away.

'I'm s-sorry…' she gulped, but that confession of his had set free the pent-up tears as nothing else could have done.

'I've been tough on you,' Rauf conceded, and then he questioned why he had said that, but he did not question why he was holding her for that development struck him as inevitable.

'It's hardly your fault that Brett's a total creep,' Lily bit out unsteadily, giving way to what every natural sense prompted and pushing forward into the support of his broad muscled chest to bury her damp face in his shoulder. 'But I don't want to think about him right now.'

'I expect not.' Rauf held her back from him and used one lean hand to tip her lovely face back up to his.

It was the optimum moment to demand answers. His other hand closed into the fall of her hair where a clip held it confined. His intent golden eyes melded with her damp blue gaze for a long, timeless moment while he reminded himself that she had slept with her sister's husband, that she was an accomplished liar. But *still* he stared down into those glorious blue eyes that he recognised were the exact same shade he had chosen for the bedroom ceiling in his Istanbul apartment. A what-the-hell feeling that was totally out of character hit Rauf in a raw, energising wave.

'Why are you looking at me like that?' Lily whispered half under her breath, for he was so close she could see the gold lights in his amazing eyes and a different tension, an edge-of-seat, thrilling sense of suspense, held her taut.

'I'm appreciating you.' Rauf tilted her back over one strong arm as he freed the clip confining the long, thick fall of her hair and tossed it aside. He made every move with exaggerated slowness, instinctively waiting for her to protest or retreat as she had once done whenever he got too close. Her response in his arms the day before still struck him as unreal, for that was not how he remembered her.

Beneath the burning probe of Rauf's measuring appraisal, she felt her breath feather in her throat for she could hardly wait to feel his mouth on hers again. 'Are you?'

'Very much…' Rauf husked, a bitter sort of amusement lancing through him, for there was no doubt in his mind now that the reluctance he had met with before could only have been a deliberate ploy to make him all the keener. 'Especially as you don't seem quite so nervous as you used to be around me.'

Hot pink surged into Lily cheeks and her uneasy gaze dropped from his in embarrassment at that unexpected reminder. 'I got over that.'

But *when* had she magically got over it? Just yesterday when she'd appreciated that he held the future of Harris Travel in his hand? Dark, dangerous thoughts threatening, Rauf tuned them out with single-minded purpose and let his fingers slide into her gorgeous hair to tug the golden weight of glossy strands round her taut shoulders where it coiled and slid downward again in a tumbling mass. 'I always wanted to see you wear it loose like this.'

'It's too long…gets in the way.' The smouldering entrapment of his golden gaze kept her still. She could hardly breathe and her heart was thumping as though she had run a marathon, making it difficult for her to speak. Her breasts ached and a liquid sensation of heat was stirring at the very heart of her so that she pressed her thighs together in sudden guilty mortification.

'I love it…' Rauf confided thickly, dropping his lean, strong hands to her slender hips to raise her to him. 'I promise you…it won't get in *my* way.'

He captured her lips in a slow, searching onslaught that sent her senses spinning. The very taste of him was pure intoxication and the feel of his sensual mouth sublime. All that still approached rational thought was stolen from her in the first few seconds and then the sheer pleasure of what he was doing to her took over. He explored the tender interior of her mouth with a seductive expertise that made her gasp and cling, fingers biting into his broad shoulders with helpless impatience, tiny little tremors assailing her quivering length while she melted and burned for more.

Rauf lifted his dark head. 'Time to make a move…' he growled, springing upright.

Before she had even surfaced from the effects of that last lingering kiss, he had bent and swept her up into his arms to stride across the *basoda* and into a connecting hallway.

Lily stole a confused ennervated look up at Rauf. 'I can walk…'

'I like carrying you,' Rauf imparted with a slashing smile that brought his lean, devastating features to vibrant, charismatic life.

Her heart leapt inside her at the appeal of that smile.

Rauf shot a charged glance down at her. 'I'm taking you to my bed, *güzelim*. If you don't like that idea, say so now…'

Something akin to panic seized Lily in initial response to that invitation. His bed. Wasn't it much too soon for that development? But was she about to refuse the only male who had *ever* managed to make her want him? Taking into account his strong pride and their past history, he would never approach her again. This time around he expected an adult relationship and evidently he saw no reason why they shouldn't just go straight to bed. Having stuck by her moral principles would be cold consolation if she lost Rauf again at their expense. And, all nerves and shyness aside, if she was truly honest with herself, the mere idea of finding out what real passion was like with Rauf just left her limp and weak with wanton, wicked longing.

'Lily…?' Rauf prompted, strung high on the suspicion that he had fallen for yet another come-on destined to end in a freezing-cold shower.

Lily collided with sizzling golden eyes and butterflies broke loose in her tummy. By dint of clutching his shoulder, she lifted herself up to find his tempting mouth again for herself and gave him her answer that way. He succumbed with a roughened groan of appreciation and flattering immediacy. It was at least a minute before Lily got a single brain cell operating again and by that stage she was being set down on a superb gilded and carved bed. Instant tension froze her there.

Rauf backed off just to fully enjoy the sight of her there on his bed, her wonderful hair draped round her in a rippling sheet of gold, fairy-tale-princess style. She looked breathtaking. As he shed his jacket where he stood, quite unable as yet to actually imagine touching her, his tawny gaze rested on her and narrowed with sudden decisive force.

He was going to *keep* her! No way was he letting her go again. Why should his moral code sentence him to self-denial in his private life? He would take her back to Istanbul and set her up there in an apartment. In a cosmopolitan city, such arrangements were understood. If a faint current of unease assailed Rauf on the score that his female relatives were about as sophisticated as home-baked bread and as quick to pick up on gossip about him as high-tech listening devices, he blocked it out fast. At the age of thirty, he told himself that he had an indisputable right to live his life as he saw fit.

'I can't take my eyes off you…' Rauf confessed with roughened appreciation.

Lily watched him jerk loose his silk tie and let it fall and her tension level hit another high. She could not take her eyes from him either, but then nor could she quite believe that she was on his bed so soon after her arrival in Turkey. She felt terrifyingly shy and self-conscious yet being with Rauf still felt so right to her. But then he had stayed in her heart, hadn't he? Her memory of him locked there with magnetic determination and ferocious staying power. Taken aback by a truth that she had denied for so long, Lily focused on Rauf with dawning comprehension and understood why her resistance was nil around him. She had never got over loving him.

'Do you do this all the time?' Lily heard herself ask without even being aware that she was about to frame such a leading question.

Halfway through unbuttoning his shirt, Rauf stilled in surprise.

'I mean...' Lily continued unsteadily, her tongue reacting to her anxious thoughts faster than caution could instigate a hold on it. '...just kiss and go straight to...er... bed?'

'Not since I was a teenager.' Somehow, Rafe acknowledged a second later, that was not the most comforting of thoughts.

Her cheeks flushed, Lily bent her golden head. 'I just wondered.'

Without hesitation, Rauf gathered her up and kissed her with drugging intensity. 'This is *us*...that's different,' he pointed out.

Stepping back from her, he peeled off his shirt. Lips tingling but mouth running dry, Lily stared: he was all sleek, rippling muscles and bronzed skin. He was magnificent. A haze of dark curls outlined his pectorals and arrowed down into a faint furrow over his flat, taut abdomen. As he embarked on removing his well-cut trousers, treating her to a view of his narrow waist, lean hips and a disturbing glimpse of long, powerful, hair-roughened thighs, Lily actually thought she might have a heart attack then and there. Dragging in a stark sudden breath, she dredged her attention from him, but his disturbing image stayed stamped behind her eyelids: incredibly male, big, dominating. Rampantly sexy too, just rather panic-inducing.

'I forgot to offer you lunch...' Rauf commented without warning.

'Lunch?' Lily echoed as the mattress gave beneath his added weight. Without glancing in his direction, she endeavoured to look less like a reclining statue. Having watched his boxer shorts hit the rug, she wasn't quite ready as yet to embrace the visual challenge of him in all his unadorned glory.

'Later...' Rauf promised, closing a long, confident arm round her to tug her back towards him, shift her hair out of his path and reach for the zip on her dress.

Lily almost told him she was too hungry to wait for lunch. Only will-power kept her on the bed. Hadn't she passed the kissing category with flying colours? Why else had they reached the bed so fast? Only Rauf was now expecting her to jump several categories all at once and without any prior practice. This was Rauf she was with, though, she reminded herself bracingly. He would make the experience as good as it could be. Adverse circumstances challenged him, brought out the very best in his competitive character.

'This feels so sexy...' he purred, inching down her zip only inch by inch, dragging out the moment as befitted what felt like an historic occasion, for he had never seen an inch of Lily exposed between throat and knee.

'Does it?' Lily muttered tautly as cooler air touched her spine.

'You have incredibly soft skin.' Lean fingers brushing

over her narrow back, Rauf let his lips zero in on the pale perfection of one slender shoulder and linger there.

His knowing mouth felt like a brand on her and she trembled, suddenly plunged back into aching awareness. Weak with longing, she leant back into him for support. But instead, he turned her round to face him, took her lush mouth with hungry urgency and drove every thought from her mind. Her dress and her bra fell to the carpet without her even being aware of their smooth removal. Every inch of her skin felt supersensitive, thrumming with wild antic-ipation to the passionate melding of his mouth on hers and the even more erotic plunge of his tongue. Nothing else existed for her, nothing else mattered, and she laced her fingers into the springy depths of his hair to hold him to her.

But when Rauf drew back and lifted her to pull the bedspread back from beneath her and settle her on the cool crisp sheet instead, the real world reclaimed Lily again. As she tumbled back against the feather pillows she was star-tled to find herself clad in only her panties and embar-rassment inflamed her at the sight of her own bare breasts.

But Rauf wasted no time in coming back to her again, smouldering golden eyes raking over her with very male appreciation.

'You're gorgeous,' he breathed with roughened convic-tion as he absorbed the picture she made against the white linen: blue eyes bright as stars, her lips reddened from his, her glorious hair semi-veiling her in sensual disarray, al-lowing only a tantalising glimpse of one pouting, pink-tipped breast. With Lily in his life, getting out of bed to make an early meeting would prove to be the toughest challenge he had ever faced. But also the most enjoyable.

Heart hammering at the charged appraisal she was receiving, Lily parted dry lips. 'I should warn you...I still haven't...er...done this before.'

Taken aback by that unlikely claim, Rauf screened his sardonic gaze and tried not to wince for her. Surely she didn't *still* expect him to believe that she was pure as driven snow? But then, as he had chosen not to confront her about her liaison with Gilman, she might feel that she had to keep up that pretence. But even after several years had passed?

In the taut silence, Lily worried anxiously at her lower lip. 'Does that put you off?'

'Nothing could do that.' Relieved that she had said something he could answer with honesty, Rauf took the easy way out. Bringing her back to him again, he crushed her inviting mouth under his own and kissed her breathless.

Reeling from that impassioned onslaught, Lily lay back in his arms, quivering at the hot, hard weight and lure of his muscular body lying half over hers. She collided with shimmering golden eyes as he moulded the tender swell of her breasts and her spine arched, pushing her sensitised flesh up into shameless, satisfying contact with his palms. Sweet sensation fired her with a wicked, restive impatience that embarrassed her. Without pause, he captured a straining pink nipple between his lips and an audible gasp was dragged from her. An insistent throb had begun at the very heart of her. Suddenly her body was in control of her, desperate and hungry for more of that tormenting pleasure and unable to conceal the fact.

'Never have I wanted a woman as I want you now,' Rauf admitted with a ragged edge to his dark drawl. It was the truth, but a truth he bitterly resented.

But that confession thrilled Lily and her eyes shone and she had not a doubt in her head from that moment that she was doing the right thing: giving where once she had been afraid to give and sharing in the same way. 'It's the same for me,' Lily whispered, looking up at him with complete trust.

Only it had not always been the way and Rauf was all too well aware of that fact. A dangerous smile curved his expressive mouth. 'Now that Brett's gone?'

Lily blinked, unable to grasp the connection and then suddenly wondering in shrinking dismay if Rauf had suspected all along that there was something odd about her relationship with her sister's ex-husband. But she shrank from the idea of telling Rauf about Brett's loathsome behaviour towards her when she had been a teenager. Brett might never have touched her, but he had left her feeling soiled and she was convinced that Rauf would be disgusted, repulsed...or, worse, that he might even wonder if in some way she might have invited or encouraged that attention from the other man. Either way, she believed that Rauf would think very much less of her.

'Sorry...I don't follow,' Lily muttered in a discomfited rush.

She was pale, blue eyes awash with strain and conflict that Rauf interpreted as guilt. A guilt that gave him no satisfaction but that sent sudden ferocious anger flaring through him. If he ever got his hands on Gilman, he knew he would hammer the bastard into a pulp.

Veiling his fierce, glittering scrutiny, he just pushed himself up and reached out to yank Lily back across the small space that separated them into his arms again.

'It may be a big bed,' Rauf quipped, 'but that doesn't mean you're allowed to stray.'

It was pure caveman but she melted into the lean, hard heat and strength of his muscular frame. Even as relief that he had not said any more about Brett washed over her every nerve-ending she possessed went on red alert at the renewed force of desire that overwhelmed her that close to him.

She burned with a helpless mix of nerves and anticipation as she felt the hot, hard length of his arousal against her belly. He rearranged her, teased the throbbing peaks of her breasts with his tongue until she writhed and gasped, and she was lost in sensation again long before he sought out the slick dampness between her slender thighs. He caressed the most sensitive spot of all and she moaned out loud, startled by her own feverish response. The intensity kept on building until she was panting for breath, pitched to a torment of wanting by his merest touch.

'Rauf…' she gasped, and she didn't even know what she wanted to say, only that the hunger was almost unbearable, the ache consuming her a growing torture to withstand.

Scorching desire blazed in the golden eyes that scanned her as he donned protection. He sank his hands beneath her squirming hips and came over her in one lithe move. He entered her with a smooth, expert thrust and wanton little tremors of pleasure assailed her at that initial sensation of his fullness stretching her tight.

Then he said something in his own language, surprise darkening his heated gaze as he had to lift her and tip her up further to sheathe himself in her fully. A sharp stab of pain jolted Lily at the height of that manoeuvre and for a split second she went rigid and wasn't quite quick enough to bite back a startled yelp of complaint.

Rauf felt that resistance too late. He stopped, in fact he froze as if a fire alarm had gone off, but his own powerful momentum had already carried him through that delicate barrier. 'Lily…?' and his voice just failed him for the first time in his life.

'It's all right,' Lily mumbled dizzily, adjusting with admirable speed, ease and appreciation to a category of sensation that her body sensed harboured the promise of possibilities she had not even dreamt might exist. 'I'm getting used to it…*oh*…oh, yes…'

Eyes tight shut, Lily wrapped both arms round him, shifted her hips experimentally and was seized by such a blinding wave of delicious sensation that she was left breathless and craving more. Hunger for her reignited to fever pitch but, fighting it, Rauf moved to withdraw, but she arched up to him in encouragement and at that point he succumbed by sinking back into her with an earthy groan. Her excitement mounted with every fluid thrust of his lithe body into hers, his primal rhythm driving her pleasure to uncontrollable heights. Then she hit a glorious peak and broke up into a million tiny, ecstatically happy little pieces. She coasted down from that dazzling experience with a sense of profound wonderment.

Tension would not allow Rauf to reach the same rewarding climax. He withdrew and stared down at her happy, *innocent* face and it was like having a knife plunged into him to the hilt. Releasing her from his weight, he rolled over. Lily scooted back into connection with him, dropped a kiss on the bunched muscles of one wide shoulder, drank in the sexy scent of his damp, hot skin with dizzy satisfaction and the heady sense of being a *real* woman. Rauf flipped back, curved an arm round her slight length and drew her close again.

'I feel so…so happy,' Lily finally admitted, still on a self-preoccupied high unlike any she had ever experienced. The world at just that moment encompassed Rauf and there it stopped. She was in his arms. She loved him. She had finally made it into bed with him and been rewarded beyond her wildest hopes.

'I need a shower...' Rauf breathed grittily.

And as Lily opened her eyes to watch Rauf stride towards the door on the far wall she noticed, really could not have helped noticing, that *he* was still...unsatisfied. The sheer extent of her own alarming ignorance of why that should be preoccupied her. Her sunny sense of achievement died there. Only then did she recall that in the aftermath of their lovemaking he had initially pulled away from her, had not spoken, had indeed only put his arms round her after she had swarmed all over him first.

A hollow, sick sensation in her tummy, Lily sat up and hugged her knees, anxious eyes dark with pain and mortification. Obviously, Rauf hadn't got much of a thrill from taking her to bed and, even though he had still been aroused, he hadn't wanted to continue either. That latter fact seemed the lowest blow of all. The shower seemed to exert more charisma than she did. Why, though? What had she done wrong?

CHAPTER FIVE

RAUF was having a very long cold shower.

Lily had been a virgin. Rauf was still transfixed by the shock value of that discovery. In fact, he was so stunned by that revelation and by the equally disturbing experience of having been proven wrong in his every conviction that it was an intellectual challenge just to surmount that and move on into more practical mode of what to do next. He would have to be honest with her. That was his first decision.

He then attempted to picture a scene in which he would tell Lily that he had once believed that she was sleeping with her sister's husband. What was more, he had believed that of her right up until he had shared a bed with her himself. Rauf grimaced. No, he definitely didn't want to run with the unvarnished truth. She would be horrified and offended beyond forgiveness. How could he distress her by admitting that he had credited the existence of such a *very* sleazy affair? That he had ditched her because of that same belief? That he had believed she had betrayed not only his trust, but also her own sister's?

And all the time, Lily had been all that she herself claimed to be, everything she had seemed on first acquaintance and everything he had once accepted her as being. So, when she came off with things like, 'Can't we still be friends?', she really, truly *meant* it. In the cleanest sense. That had not been a subtle sexual hint that this time around she was willing to spread herself on his bed.

At that point, Rauf groaned out loud, raked long brown

fingers through his wet black hair. A dozen once strictly censored and cynically dissected and despoilt memories bombarded him in their restored and original form. Memories of Lily that summer before they broke up. In all of those recollections, Lily featured as being especially nice, especially soft-hearted and especially unmaterialistic.

For a start, she just adored little children and lavished phenomenal patience on even the irritating yappy ones. She was a pushover for every tramp or homeless person that came within twenty feet of her and she had cried when he'd told her about his dog dying when he was eleven. She had even worried that he was spending too much money on her and had kept on making up picnics so that they could eat alfresco. It was getting very cold in the shower but Rauf was looking back three years in time with an unfamiliar sense of appalled bewilderment at the colossal depth of his own misconceptions about Lily. Shivering, he finally grabbed a towel.

The more he examined his own behaviour, the worse it seemed. He got no brownie points on any score. At every juncture, he had assumed worst-case scenario and treated her accordingly. Therefore, candour really wasn't a viable option. Off that particularly challenging hook, Rauf breathed again. She never had known the way his mind had worked and now he knew that he never, ever wanted her to find out. He was a ruthless, cynical guy with, it seemed, a mind as naturally given over to intrigue and seething suspicion of his woman as that Shakespeare character who had done away with his wife. He didn't want any living soul knowing that and Lily, who scared easy, least of all!

Just one small inconsistency continued to nag at him. What *had* she been doing in that hotel with Brett Gilman? And why had she lied about being there? Furthermore, why had she stopped being so nervous around him? What miracle had brought about that refreshing change? Quit wondering stuff like that, Rauf's new caution control centre warned him. He strode through the connecting door to the dressing-room and yanked out fresh clothes. Lily looks like an angel, she *is* an angel, stop doubting your good fortune at landing the one woman you do not deserve to have!

As Lily listened to Rauf's shower running, she told herself that she would get up and get dressed in just a minute. Lying in his bed naked now felt shameless and all her intoxication with her own daring had shrivelled on the vine. Foolish love and even sillier hopes had led her astray and she hadn't had to wait long to pay a price for her stupidity. Why didn't she just face it? All Rauf had ever wanted from her was sex and, having finally got it, he had been disappointed.

But then, one way or another, hadn't she always disappointed him? Her mind roamed back to when she had first met Rauf Kasabian…

The glorious flowers he had sent in apology for the fracas over the red wine being spilt had merely heralded Rauf's reappearance at the bar later that same day. He'd wasted no time either in making his intentions clear. Throwing back his handsome dark head, he had treated her to that riveting smile of his and murmured, 'I think we both know I'm only here to see you again.'

'But you have a girlfriend—'

'No…I don't date women who scream at other women in public. I'll wait until you finish your shift.'

Never had she met a male less aware of the possibility of rejection. Automatic refusal trembled on her lips but remained unspoken, for when she met his gorgeous dark golden eyes the thought of him walking away and never coming back just silenced her. When she had to serve the table beside Rauf's, a drunk put his hand on her bottom and she brushed it away. When the drunk then asked her who the hell she thought she was, Rauf intervened.

'She's mine,' Rauf drawled with perfect equanimity. 'So hands off…'

He took her back to her apartment in a taxi to get changed and Annabel followed Lily into her tiny bedroom to snipe, 'All right, so you're *not* gay and you've snagged him. But that guy will expect more than a hug at the end of the night, so don't say you weren't warned!'

'Meaning?' Lily was apprehensive enough without that assurance.

'He's a real sexy stud. It's written all over him. Enjoy yourself tonight because you won't see him again,' Annabel forecast. 'You'll say no. He won't waste any more time on you…after all, why should he? Girls always come across for guys like him.'

He took her to dine in a wonderful Turkish restaurant and they talked for hours. Well, mostly he talked and she listened. He was working on the launch of a news magazine and he would be in London all summer. That first night he didn't even try to kiss her but he booked her every free hour for the entire week ahead.

The second night he did kiss her but she coped because it was broad daylight and in a public place and she did not feel threatened in any way. She also discovered that she liked it when he kissed her. The third night, he asked her to come back to his hotel and spend the night with him, as if sharing her body with a male she had only known a couple of days was the most natural thing in the world.

'I don't do stuff like that,' she told him.

'Of course you do,' Rauf traded. 'You're only trying to

play that time-honoured female game…make him desperate before you say yes. But I was desperate within seconds of first laying eyes on you.'

'I haven't ever slept with anyone,' Lily finally mumbled.

There was a very long silence. Startled tawny eyes gazed deep into hers. 'You're saying you're *a*…?'

Hurriedly she nodded, face flaming.

'I suppose I ought to say that seducing virgins isn't my style but, to be very frank,' Rauf husked, those smouldering eyes turning slumbrous with anticipation, 'I've never been in this situation before and the idea of being your first lover just blows my mind!'

That was not the understanding response she had been hoping to receive and she muttered in considerable embarrassment, 'What I'm trying to say is that I really want to wait until I'm married.'

'But I'm not looking for a wife. I doubt that I'll ever marry,' Rauf informed her steadily. 'I come from a family where for several generations marriage at a very young age was the norm. I've been fending off potential brides since I was eighteen. I like my freedom. So if you want more, I'm the wrong guy.'

She wished he had told her all that on the first date. By then it was too late to stop loving him. But the night died there and at the end of it she told him she didn't want to see him again. And, even now, she remembered the dark, incredulous fury in his lean, devastating features and the fright it had given her to see what a temper he had. He hadn't said or done anything to demonstrate that anger but that memory had lingered. For forty-eight hours, he didn't call and then he turned up at the bar, still furious with her but trying to hide it and, just looking at him, she knew that, even if their relationship had no future, he was still her fate. That same week he found her another job as a receptionist in a beauty salon owned by the wife of a friend of his and she was very grateful.

For a few weeks, they had a wonderful time together most of the time. Things only went wrong when sex entered the equation. On three separate occasions, she steeled herself to go back to his hotel with him. The first time, he said to her, 'You're not ready for this,' because when he tried to move beyond kissing she just froze on him. The second time she drank too much in the hope of losing her inhibitions and he took her home in brooding silence. The third time, she told him he made her feel scared sometimes and he looked so shaken she felt the most awful guilt because she knew that she was the one with the problem, not him.

But then, surprisingly, for a while, he just accepted how she was and he was very gentle and caring and she loved him more than ever. Yet when Hilary begged her to bring Rauf home, she continued to make excuses. Then Brett turned up at her student flat one night just before Rauf was due to pick her up.

'It's time we buried the hatchet,' Brett announced with a creepy smile while she shrank behind the door and kept it on the chain. 'Hilary is gasping to meet this Rauf Kasabian character and I swear I'll be on my best behaviour if you bring him home for the weekend.'

'Why? Why would you swear that?'

'Hilary's hurt that you hardly ever visit. That makes me feel bad.'

Rauf was amazingly keen to meet her family and, although she was surprised by his interest in investing in Harris Travel, it was a terrific weekend. A week later, they made a second visit because Rauf's accountant had flown over from Turkey to look at Harris Travel's accounts and the contract Rauf's London lawyer had already drawn up in readiness was then signed by Rauf and her father. But during those same forty-eight hours, everything that could go wrong *did* go wrong...

Lily was very much on edge with the knowledge that Rauf was within days of making a permanent return to Turkey. Her niece, Gemma, was ill when they arrived. Lily had to offer to stand in for a sick member of staff the following day at the travel agency. Then, Gemma was taken into hospital for emergency surgery and Hilary was frantic and unable to contact Brett. Shutting out that unappealing slice of memory, Lily remembered how she had seen Rauf off at the airport that same evening and not one word had he said about seeing her again or not seeing her again or indeed anything else. But that had been the last time she'd seen or heard from him. Once she had called his mobile phone just to check he was still alive and he had answered and she had not had the nerve to speak.

When Rauf strode back into the bedroom, Lily gave him an aghast look for she had lost track of time. Having intended to be dressed and elsewhere by the time he reappeared, she just dived under the sheet like a little kid, leaving nothing but some trailing hair showing.

Rauf was very encouraged by the fact that Lily was still in his bed an hour after the event. In particular, an event that had been a lot less of an event than it should have been. She was still naked too, which meant she was a captive audience.

'Lily...'

'Go away...I want to get dressed!' Lily launched from below the sheet, feeling exceedingly foolish.

Rauf hunkered down by the side of the bed, inched up the sheet about three inches and met frantic blue eyes. 'I've been a total inconsiderate bastard but I *do* care about you.'

'Prove it then…go away!' Lily urged chokily, thinking that that noncommittal word, 'care' had always come very readily to Rauf's lips around her. But that word promised nothing and while she'd waited on a phone that had never rung at the age of twenty-one she had learned the hard way that his concept of 'caring' could mean absolutely nothing too.

'I can't stand it when you're upset and you won't let me hold you!' Rauf fired back at her in immediate frustration.

At that, Lily lifted her head a little. He sounded so sincere. 'I just don't understand you….'

'Why would you even want to?' Rauf asked her, gathering strength by the second on that reassuring piece of news. 'I'm a guy. I'm supposed to be different.'

'You're *too* different,' Lily told him helplessly. 'I don't know where I am with you.'

'In my bed beneath my sheet and I'm going to rip you out of there if you don't come out under your own steam,' Rauf told her steadily.

Fierce resentment hurtled up through Lily. 'You do that…and I promise you, I'll thump you!'

Dark golden eyes arrowed over her angry face in astonishment at that threat. 'I was only teasing…'

No, she knew he hadn't been. On that level, she knew him well. Ripping off the sheet would not have cost Rauf a second of hesitation. He was a stranger to patience.

Lily shimmied up from under the sheet, carrying it carefully with her until her head hit the pillows again. She didn't even think about what she was doing because with every moment that passed a far more engrossing conviction had been growing on her. It was as if time had gone into reverse. It was spooky. Somehow, somewhere between vacating the bedroom and returning to it, Rauf had switched back into being the male she remembered him being in London. More relaxed, less abrasive, not a shade of coldness or scorn or reserve about him and there was warmth in his beautiful eyes again. So what had changed? No matter how hard she tried, she could not stop staring at him.

It was a bad move, she conceded dizzily because, as usual, Rauf looked drop-dead gorgeous. Sheathed in black jeans, he could have sold racks of them to besotted women and his grey tee shirt was designer casual and made him seem much more approachable than a business suit did. And then there was him, the guy in the clothes. Black hair still damp from the shower, the riveting attraction of that lean, hard-boned face and the dark, deepset eyes with only a restive glitter of gold pinned to her with an intensity she could feel.

Rauf sank down on the edge of the bed and spread two lean brown hands. 'I was *really* surprised that you were a virgin. I know you said you were but I didn't believe you.'

At that sudden confession, Lily blinked in slow motion. 'You mean...you *never* believed me?'

'I did when we first met...most of the time,' he qualified, opting for total truth on that score. 'But sometimes I did wonder if it was just a clever way of trying to wring a marriage proposal out of me.'

Lily lost colour and studied him in frank reproach even as resentment made her bridle. 'You told me how you felt about marriage. I knew that what we had was going nowhere.'

Strangely enough, that concluding statement annoyed the hell out of Rauf.

'There was nowhere for it *to* go,' Lily continued helplessly, wondering why his stubborn jawline had clenched as if she had said something offensive. 'I lived in England. You lived here. All that was on offer was a casual affair.'

'I don't do casual,' Rauf drawled, brilliant golden eyes challenging.

Her lush mouth tightened and her lashes screened her gaze, her lovely face shadowing. 'You just *did*...here, with me,' she breathed unsteadily, her throat tightening because talking about anything so intimate did not come easily to her. 'I don't know what I expected, but it wasn't the way you behaved afterwards—'

Rauf leant forward, closed one hand over hers. 'I told you that I—'

'That you were totally wrapped up in yourself as usual,' Lily sliced in helplessly.

Hugely disconcerted by that condemnation, Rauf tightened his lean brown fingers over hers. 'That's *not* what I said—'

'But what it comes down to. You didn't *care*...' Lily framed painfully. 'About how I felt that you were disappointed.'

'*Disappointed?* Is that what you think?' Rauf demanded in disbelief, 'totally wrapped up in yourself as usual' still lingering with a sting he couldn't believe and keen to shift the dialogue into safer channels. 'How could you think I was disappointed with you?'

'I don't want to discuss that...' Lily became very evasive when it came to the point of sharing how she had reached that conclusion.

Lacing his other hand into her hair, Rauf tugged her forward and devoured her mouth with a passionate hunger that had a megawatt effect on her startled system. Heart banging fit to burst, pulses racing, Lily looked up at Rauf with stunned eyes as he sprang upright, peeled off his tee shirt over his head and unzipped his jeans.

'Rauf…?' Lily whispered in a daze.

The boxer shorts landed in a heap beside the discarded jeans. Glorious as a Greek god, he had the additional appeal of being infinitely more hot-blooded for he sported a bold erection. Lily flushed to the roots of her hair but a wanton little throb thrummed deep down inside her in response.

'Could I persuade you to disappoint me again?' Rauf asked with sizzling effect.

Lily sort of slid down the bed into a more encouraging position without even thinking about it and ten seconds later Rauf was melded to her like a second skin. And if the first time had struck her as incredible, the second time qualified as wild. Afterwards, she fell asleep in his arms floating high above planet earth, got woken up to disappoint him again at some length. Then with a boundless energy that could only impress her when she honestly thought she would never move again, he answered a phone call, pulled on his clothes, said he'd order dinner for them and that he had to return that call. From the door, he gazed back at her, vibrant golden eyes centring on her again and he strode back, threw himself down on the bed to extract a last lingering kiss and groaned out loud at having to drag himself away.

'Later…' he promised huskily.

The sun was going down behind the shutters when Lily tottered out of bed to take advantage of his shower. She felt like a woman lost in an erotic dream. She felt sublime. He made her feel so loved. Wasn't that strange? It was only sexual love. She knew that, of course she did. She told herself that she was not naive enough to start thinking that Rauf's incredible passion for her body meant anything more. But she was awash with images of having been held close and showered in endless compliments too.

'You're exquisite...' he had said.

'You're perfect for me...' he had sighed.

'I find you irresistible...'

For the moment, Lily affixed, reflecting back to that last assurance. She was in love with a male who would never regard her as anything more than a small part of his life, who would never say the love word even under torture and who would always be very, very careful to promise nothing he could not deliver.

Rauf had once described the staunchly traditional Kasabian family to her and Lily sighed at the ironic damage that that trio of matriarchal figures—his great-grandmother, grandmother and mother—had done to their own fondest hopes of marrying him off. For a start, Rauf had been educated at an English public school and literally raised between two different cultures.

But when he was eighteen his family had begun inviting over the daughters of family friends and business acquaintances and telling him that he didn't need to get married for a few years but that there was no harm in choosing early and settling on a long engagement. Over-protective of him, no doubt aware that with his looks and wealth he would be targeted by designing women in droves, his female relatives had been desperate to get him safely welded to some suitable girl even before he'd gone to university. Of course, given Rauf's force of character and stubborn nature, all that pressure had had the exact opposite effect. Staying single had become a burning crusade.

When she returned to the bedroom, she discovered that her case had been brought up. Having dried her hair, she was in the act of clipping it back when she recalled Rauf's preference and then, smiling, she left it loose. As she put on a pale green cotton skirt and a fitted, short-sleeved white shirt she thought about how much stronger she had grown since she was sixteen. At sixteen, naively believing that her long blonde hair was responsible for drawing Brett's attention to her, she had gone out one Saturday and had it cut to within two inches of her skull. Hilary had been shocked but Brett had just laughed and had continued to target her. Apart from the occasional trim, Lily now wore her hair long in defiance of the timid teenager she had once been. But she would wear it loose only for Rauf's pleasure.

Rauf was in the main room in the old part of the house still talking on the phone. His lean, strong face flashed into a brilliant smile of welcome that left her giddy. He closed an arm round her, finished his call and led her outside to a charming old stone-built arbour lit with lanterns that overlooked the lush gardens. Drinks and an astonishing variety of appetisers on tiny plates were brought by a man-servant.

'*Mucver*…courgette. *Piyaz*…that is haricot and this one is *sigara boregi*…cheese pastries.' Explaining what each was, Rauf encouraged Lily to try a little of everything and he watched her enjoyment of Turkish cuisine with unconcealed pride.

It was a fantastic meal. Even Rauf seemed taken aback by the number of courses that appeared and the wide selection of dishes.

'Do you eat like this every night?' Lily could not help asking.

'Not unless it's a special occasion.' Rauf shook his proud dark head and laughed. 'This feast can only be in honour of my guest. As Sonngul is remote, it is rare for me to entertain here but to offer the ultimate in hospitality is a matter of pride to all Turkish people.'

He asked her about the nursery school where she worked and she told him about the children she taught. Having eaten, however, she began to feel guilty that even a few hours had passed without her pressing Rauf to a task that surely ought to be tackled as soon as possible. The sooner Rauf acquired the evidence he wanted to prove Brett's guilt, the sooner Hilary could be told about the disastrous financial losses about to engulf the travel agency.

'Perhaps we could take a look at Harris Travel's bank statements and stuff now,' Lily suggested rather awkwardly.

A wry smile curved his beautiful, sensual mouth. 'I have no need of your assistance in that line, *güzelim*.'

'But isn't that why you brought me here?' Lily queried in surprise. 'To *help*?'

'That was an excuse,' Rauf admitted. 'On my behalf, discreet enquiries are already being made through the head office of that Turkish bank in London. I have considerable influence and in due course the confidential information that I require will be given to me.'

That smooth explanation shook Lily, for she had never dreamt that his invitation to Sonngul might not be what it had seemed. 'You don't need me at all?'

'How can you ask me that when you met my *every* need this afternoon?' The irreverent look of shameless intimacy in Rauf's dark golden gaze fired hot pink across Lily's troubled and increasingly weary face. 'But as I have already told you, I didn't want you muddying the waters of my investigation either.'

'You're very clever at concealing your true motives,' Lily remarked tightly.

'Our situation has changed since our first meeting at the Aegean Court. I didn't trust you then,' Rauf reminded her levelly. 'But I still want the evidence that will nail Gilman's hide to the wall. I make no apology for that.'

Lily sighed heavily. 'I'd dearly like to see him punished too but…that's going to hurt my family a lot.'

'I'm afraid there's no room for negotiation on the prosecution front.' Rauf's jawline squared. 'But I see no reason why your family should suffer too.'

'But they *will* suffer,' Lily muttered painfully. 'There's nothing you can do about that.'

Rauf looked amused. 'Of course there is…I won't allow your family to be ruined. I'll just refinance Harris Travel.'

In receipt of that extraordinarily generous proposition, Lily stiffened in astonishment. She also found herself wondering if that offer was the direct result of her having met his 'every need' in bed. It was a demeaning thought, which made it impossible for her to continue meeting his eyes. 'Neither Dad or Hilary could accept that. You've lost money and they've lost money but Harris Travel is *our* business and responsibility and Brett was Hilary's husband.'

'I'll deal with it. You don't need to worry about anything.' With cool assurance, Rauf stroked a light forefinger in a soothing caress across the back of her clenched hand where it rested on the table. 'I'll take care of it all. Trust me.'

Still in turmoil from the shock of that offer of further cash support, Lily tugged her hand shakily free and stood up. 'If I promise not to contact anyone, will you have me taken back to my hotel?'

In one lithe movement, Rauf sprang upright. 'But why should you want to leave?'

'Because I feel that what happened between us today… and this horrible situation with Brett are getting much too tangled up together!'

But before she could walk back into the house, Rauf stepped into her path. A lean hand pushed up her chin.

Keen dark golden eyes searched her strained face. 'You don't want Brett prosecuted,' he condemned in a tone so chilling that Lily trembled.

'I do…it's you who doesn't understand—'

'*Make* me,' he urged.

As briefly as she could, Lily explained how much her family had already endured in recent times: Joy's long illness, which had worn Hilary to the bone, the loss of the Harris home in the divorce settlement, Douglas Harris's subsequent depression. Rauf's lean, handsome features grew even more grim as he listened to that recital of woes, all of them brought about or exacerbated by Brett Gilman's monstrous lack of concern for his own children.

'But there's no way that Hilary or my father would accept more money from you,' Lily reiterated in a driven undertone. 'And I don't want to listen to you offer that just because I…I slept with you! Can't you see how that makes me feel?'

'No. What you see is *not* what I see. You're my woman and I will look after you. There is no shame in that for you and what sort of man would I be if I didn't support you in such a crisis? I'll find a way to make my financial help acceptable to them. Call it pure selfishness, if you like. How could I stand by and do nothing while you worry about your family?'

The fierce sincerity with which Rauf voiced those arguments in his own defence and his supportive words touched Lily deep.

'You're not going back to your hotel,' he informed her, still inflamed that she could even have considered that as an option.

'But I *ought* to…' Lily groaned.

'To some degree, I'm also to blame for the freedom with which Gilman was able to steal from all of us.'

Lily frowned. 'How?'

'My last accountant was a family friend. I should've suggested that he retire much sooner than I did,' Rauf explained ruefully. 'His health was failing and the job was too demanding but still he clung to it. The very first contract payment that failed to arrive from Harris Travel should've been noted and questioned, but it wasn't.'

'That was unfortunate,' Lily conceded as Rauf walked her back indoors.

'That oversight must've encouraged Gilman to believe that he could get away with a lot more.'

Lily smothered a guilty yawn. She was so tired she might have been moving in a dream. All the unsettling events of the past forty-eight hours were weighing in on her at once.

'You're totally exhausted.' With a rueful laugh, Rauf swept her slight body up into his arms and carried her back to his bedroom, where he laid her on the bed.

The internal house phone rang and he answered it. The news that a senior officer from the *jandarma*, the section of the army responsible for law enforcement in rural areas, had driven over to Sonngul to request a meeting with him focused Rauf's thoughts fast...

CHAPTER SIX

THE older man introduced himself as Talip Hajjar and greeted Rauf with a polite apology for his intrusion.

Talip was the superior officer of the gendarme, who had prepared the file on Brett Gilman's dealings with the builders contracted to work on his villa project. From him, Rauf learned that the builders involved, having received what was owing to them from Rauf's representative, now wished to drop the charges they had laid.

'Although I understand that you have only just learned of this unpleasant business, you came forward immediately to compensate those defrauded by the Englishman. In doing so and in acknowledging your own interest in the firm who employed him, you have behaved with honour in every way. I doubt that we would ever have discovered that connection without your frank admission of it,' Talip Hajjar admitted with wry honesty. 'However, I also believe that it would be wrong to allow this dishonest foreigner to benefit from your acceptance of responsibility and escape the prosecution he deserves.'

'It is not and never was my wish that that should be the result either,' Rauf agreed with considerable gravity.

The older man regarded him with approval. 'Then I must ask you to persuade the victims of his crime to let those charges stand. They only wish to drop them out of respect for the Kasabian name. But in such circumstances, a businessman of your standing and reputation can have nothing to hide or fear.'

Unhappily, Rauf could not feel that, while he had Lily

lying in his bed, an as yet unacknowledged director of Harris Travel, that was quite true and, in instant defiance of a disturbing urge to keep quiet about her presence as a guest in his home, he offered the older man *çay*.

Over the tea that was brought, Rauf sat down to tell the gendarme officer the rest of the story. Having explained Lily's presence in Turkey, he went on to vouch for her complete ignorance of her former brother-in-law's unscrupulous activities as well as describing what her relatives had already endured at Gilman's hands.

'Her own family will face bankruptcy through this,' Rauf concluded ruefully. 'It was a sorry day indeed for the Harris family when Lily's sister married her toy-boy charmer.'

'Even their home taken from them! In placing so much trust in a son-in-law the father was sadly at fault,' Talip Hajjar contended with a grimacing shake of his head. 'And yet, which of us do not wish to place total faith in a family member?'

'If you wish to interview Lily, I would ask you to wait until tomorrow. She has already retired for the night.'

'The young woman must be very distressed at what she has discovered since her arrival. At present, I see no reason to trouble her with an official interview. However, should that situation change, I will know where to find her.'

When the officer had departed, Rauf strode back to his bedroom where he found Lily fast asleep, one hand tucked beneath the pillow, her lovely face serene above the lace neckline of the nightdress she wore. Had he not been so conscious of the faint purple shadows that lay beneath her eyes, however, he might have been tempted to waken her again. He had put his own honour on the line in standing as her character witness in an effort to shield her from being associated in any way with her corrupt former brother-in-law. He had done so gladly. But enough was enough, he told himself with decision. In turn, it was only right that Lily should explain what she had been doing at that hotel with Gilman three years earlier and, most of all, why she should've chosen to lie about it. He needed to have that last tiny shadow of doubt in her cleared away.

Around dawn after a long and restful sleep, Lily opened her eyes and focused on the light filtering in. One of the bay-window shutters had been drawn back. Rauf was sprawled along the window-seat, one powerful jean-clad thigh lifted, his attention on her as she sat up with a start.

'What's wrong?' she whispered, instantly aware of his brooding tension.

'I couldn't sleep. There's something on my mind, something I've always wanted to ask you about...'

As Rauf sprang off the seat and strolled across to the foot of the bed like a prowling lion ready to spring on the unwary, intent golden eyes zeroing in on her, Lily snatched in an anxious breath. 'I haven't quite woken up yet...but go ahead.'

'On the last occasion that I stayed at your home in England...I saw you leaving a hotel with your sister's husband.'

In stark disconcertion at that announcement, Lily lost colour and stiffened, her memory throwing her back in time to a very unpleasant experience. 'But how could you have seen me?'

'My accountant was staying at the same hotel that weekend and I had just dropped him off. I was in the car park. I watched you go in and I waited for you to come out again—'

'But if you saw me *why* didn't you mention it?' Lily studied him in growing bewilderment and annoyance. 'Why didn't you just approach me?'

'Yet you later claimed that you hadn't left the travel agency at all that morning,' Rauf completed, ignoring her interruption.

The awful silence that fell sawed at Lily's ragged nerves like a knife. But as she understood how Rauf had set her up, pure unvarnished anger lit her eyes with sapphire fire. 'So, you sat and watched me and you deliberately didn't let me know you were there. Then you encouraged me to believe that it was safe to tell a harmless fib…and all the time,' she condemned with rising volume, '*all* the time, it was a trap!'

'You lied to me…if you'd told the truth, the trap couldn't have touched you,' Rauf countered, outraged that she should dare to question his behaviour when she was the one who had been in the wrong.

Lily thrust back the sheet and threw herself out of the bed. 'Are you telling me that in your whole life you have never once told a lie to avoid embarrassment?'

His riveting golden eyes hardened. 'You're evading the issue—'

'As far as I'm concerned the real issue here is your downright devious lack of decency in setting me up to fall like that!' Lily flung. 'What about trust? What about honesty?'

'You proved yourself unworthy of my trust,' Rauf spelt out with a contempt that stung her sensitive skin like a whiplash.

As Lily snatched in a deep, quivering breath, his brilliant gaze lodged to the natural prominence and movement of her breasts as she filled her lungs with air. Her face flamed at that male sexual appraisal and, even as he looked, her weak flesh tingled and swelled and the tender peaks pinched shamefully tight. In a defensive movement, Lily folded her arms over her chest. 'Did I really?'

'Entertain me...' Rauf traded with derision. 'Give me an innocent reason for telling me that harmless little fib!'

Lily compressed her lips so hard on that invitation that pallor spread round her mouth. That day three years back she had mounted a cover-up for the sake of appearances. She had lied sooner than admit that her supposedly happy family had been, from her point of view at least, very far from being what it had seemed.

'Brett was having an affair,' Lily admitted with a bone-deep bitterness that made Rauf's gaze lock to her angry, defiant face with even keener attention. 'Not for the first time either. Unfortunately that day Hilary was desperate to get hold of him because Gemma had been rushed into hospital and he wasn't answering his mobile phone. But I had a fair idea where he would be. Local gossip suggested he always took his little tramps to the same hotel!'

'You're saying that, while you and others knew that he was a womaniser, your sister *didn't* and you chose to protect her from that knowledge?'

'Why not?' Lily tilted her chin, knowing that Rauf, whose principles had about as much bend as ice, would concede no excuse for her concealment of the truth. But she had been much too scared of what the consequences of betraying Brett might have been and of how Rauf might have reacted to the reality that Brett's threats had trapped her into keeping that silence.

'And protect him too?'

Lily sent him a furious look for daring to attack her from that angle. Her father's unswerving belief that what went on in Hilary's marriage was none of their business had been the first chain that had bound her to secrecy. 'Of course not...Brett didn't come into it...Gemma was crying for her daddy. That's *all* I cared about that day!'

'It was a hell of a long time before you came out of that hotel with Gilman,' Rauf reminded her with sardonic bite.

'Because I had Reception ring his room and nobody answered,' Lily explained with angry embarrassment. 'I checked the bar and the restaurant but he wasn't there. I didn't want to go up to the room myself and I hung about for ages, but in the end, I had to sneak past the receptionist into the lift and knock on the door of that room to get hold of him!'

Rauf found that account extraordinary, yet she told her story as though what she had done had been her only obvious choice. He could have believed that she might have chosen to stay silent the first time that she'd been confronted with her brother-in-law's infidelity. But to ask him to accept that she would turn a blind eye to more than one affair and indeed lower herself to the level of tracking Gilman down to the place where he'd been staging his adulterous tryst stretched his credulity too far. Yet he registered that Lily saw nothing strange in what she had just confessed, saw nothing questionable in her own behaviour. Yet in forewarning Gilman, she had engaged in a complicit act of protecting his position in her family circle and shielding him from the consequences that he had so richly deserved.

'Why don't you just tell me the *whole* truth? You were infatuated with Brett Gilman!' Rauf condemned with icy, derisive force.

At that shattering allegation, Lily stared back at Rauf in horror and it was a second or two before she could even get her vocal cords to work for her again. 'How can you accuse me of something that sick?'

'In what you've just told me that's the only explanation that makes sense!' Rauf shot back at her with chilling con-

GET FREE BOOKS and a FREE GIFT WHEN YOU PLAY THE...

Just scratch off the silver box with a coin. Then check below to see the gifts you get!

SLOT MACHINE GAME!

YES! I have scratched off the silver box. Please send me the 2 free Harlequin Presents® books and gift for which I qualify. I understand I am under no obligation to purchase any books, as explained on the back of this card.

106 HDL DRRZ
(H-P-01/03)

306 HDL DRRK

FIRST NAME

LAST NAME

ADDRESS

APT.#

CITY

STATE/PROV.

ZIP/POSTAL CODE

The Harlequin Reader Service® — Here's how it works:

Accepting your 2 free books and gift places you under no obligation to buy anything. You may keep the books and gift and return the shipping statement marked "cancel." If you do not cancel, about a month later we'll send you 6 additional books and bill you just $3.57 each in the U.S., or $4.24 each in Canada, plus 25¢ shipping & handling per book and applicable taxes if any.* That's the complete price and — compared to cover prices of $4.25 each in the U.S. and $4.99 each in Canada — it's quite a bargain! You may cancel at any time, but if you choose to continue, every month we'll send you 6 more books, which you may either purchase at the discount price or return to us and cancel your subscription.

*Terms and prices subject to change without notice. Sales tax applicable in N.Y. Canadian residents will be charged applicable provincial taxes and GST.

viction, his eyes cold and dark as a winter pool. 'I'm going to the *hamam* before I lose my head with you!'

The *hamam*? The bath house, she recalled abstractedly, that big domed building that she had noticed in the old courtyard and assumed to be no longer in use. There he was, the ultimate contemporary sophisticated male, about to go and immerse himself in the kind of ancient cultural experience that Hilary had urged her to try out as a tourist. As the door thudded shut in Rauf's imperious wake, Lily lifted a trembling hand to her pounding brow and sucked in a jagged breath.

You were infatuated with Brett! She shuddered in angry recoil. How very wise she had been not to tell Rauf about the distasteful treatment she had had to withstand from Brett until she had left home to attend college! No doubt, Rauf would be all too happy to construe those facts as proof of an inappropriate sexual attraction and credit his own outrageous accusation as being founded in fact.

But even aside of that concern, Lily was still in considerable shock at what Rauf had revealed about his side of events three years ago. Rauf had seen her at that hotel, had known that she had lied to him and, after she had seen him off at the airport on his flight home that same day, she had never heard from Rauf again. Was it possible that Rauf had dumped her because of that lie? At that idea, a storm of powerful emotion seized hold of Lily: anger, fierce regret, incredulous frustration. Could Rauf not understand that she had not had a choice?

No way was he taking refuge in the *hamam* where he no doubt believed that she would leave him in peace! Snatching up her light robe and pulling it on, Lily left the bedroom. Sonngul was silent and dim behind the closed shutters. Entering the old whitewashed passage that appeared to lead out to the bath house, she opened the door at the foot of it and found herself in an opulent changing room with a line of shower and changing cubicles, luxurious built-in cupboards and shelves of fleecy towels waiting in readiness. It was obvious that the facilities were still very much in current use. Shedding her nightwear, Lily yanked a bath towel from the nearest shelf, wrapped it round herself and, having opened one door to discover that it led into a massage room complete with couch, stepped through the other into the bath house itself. There she fell still in astonishment at the magnificence of her surroundings.

The giant domed roof, supported on a circle of superb marble pillars, was studded with little star-shaped glass inserts that filtered the dimness with shards of golden dawn light. The walls were a glorious rich expanse of antique tiles beneath which sat marble washing wells into which water flowed in constant refreshment. Round the perimeter of the central raised and stepped platform ran a walkway and in a further expanse a flight of steps ran down into a sizeable pool.

A towel lay abandoned there and even as she watched, Rauf's dark head broke the surface of the pool and he swam over to the steps to mount them. Nude and magnificent, water streaming from his big, powerful bronzed length and quite unaware of her presence, Rauf swept up the towel.

Her mouth running dry, Lily stared at him, watched his sleek muscles flex taut as he towelled his hair, burning colour warming her cheeks. 'Rauf...?' she breathed, disconcerted embarrassment engulfing the angry sense of frustration that had made her follow him.

In all his life, Rauf had never heard a female voice in the *hamam* and he could only be shocked. Some tourists might be willing to bathe in mixed-sex groups, but his own people were a great deal more inhibited and would not have dreamt of using even a private bath house at the same time as a member of the opposite sex. 'What are you doing in here?' he demanded, shaking out the towel and securing it round his lean hips in angry, instinctive circumspection.

Her legs uncertain supports, Lily sank down on the side of the warm central platform. 'I needed to talk to you about what you said...and *explain*—'

'And that could not have waited?' Rauf fired back at her.

'OK...once I lied to you but I want you to understand the situation as it was back then,' Lily persisted, her hands closing together in a taut movement. 'The first time I saw Brett with another woman, I was only fifteen. I told Dad about it but Dad made it quite clear that he didn't want to know and he was very angry with me—'

Taken aback by that statement, Rauf strode forward and came down by her side. 'With you? Your father was angry with *you*? But how could he be angry with you?'

'Think of how things were in our family by then,' Lily urged him heavily. 'Dad liked and trusted Brett. He'd already signed over our home to Brett and Hilary. He had allowed Brett to take on more and more responsibility at Harris Travel—'

'Your father was afraid to rock the boat,' Rauf slotted in with instant grasp of why the older man had embraced such an attitude.

'Dad believed that their marriage was their private business,' Lily confided with a helpless sob catching at her throat as her overwrought emotions threatened to get the better of her. 'Maybe to some degree he was right about that because Hilary *was* happy with Brett. She just worshipped him...she thought he was perfect but he was never faithful to her!'

Angry that he had not appreciated the complexity of the situation and that Lily should have been exposed to Gilman's sleazy habits when she was still so young and vulnerable, Rauf closed a supportive arm round her slight frame. Lily had been caught up in a sordid family secret and taught that she had to keep it quiet. That her father could have laid such a burden on her outraged Rauf, but that she should have continued to blindly respect that embargo even at the age of twenty-one and lie even to him in her efforts to cover up for Brett continued to trouble him.

'With us all still living in the same house and me feeling guilty at what I knew and what Hilary didn't know, it was horrible... I *hated* Brett and once I got away to college I hardly ever went home because I couldn't bear to be anywhere near him!' Suddenly, Lily was sobbing incoherently against Rauf, her slim figure shaking with the force of her disturbed emotions.

On the brink of asking why, if that was true, he had, prior to ever meeting her family and without even realising who the man was at the time, himself once seen Brett Gilman leaving her London apartment building, Rauf almost groaned out loud at the analytical precision of his own keen brain. So there were a few minor inconsistencies still to be cleared up, but he could not doubt the genuine pain that his angry accusation had caused and it would be cruel to probe deeper.

'I'm sorry,' Lily exclaimed raggedly. 'I'm sorry I lied to you—'

Rauf framed her distraught face with firm but gentle hands. 'It doesn't matter now...it's not worth your tears. Nothing that bastard Gilman did is worth a single tear!' Keen to distract her from the unhappy memories he had roused, Rauf lowered her down full length onto the heated navel stone and a slow smile curved his wide, sensual mouth as she looked up at him in surprise. 'Now since you are here and the rest of the household is still asleep, you might as well stay and enjoy the *hamam*.'

Lily pressed her palms down onto the surface of the marble platform beneath her and finally realised why she had been getting so warm. 'It's like a sauna...' she remarked with a soft laugh of appreciation. 'In fact this entire place is just amazing!'

Rauf lay down several feet away.

'Do the whole family bathe here together?' Lily asked.

At the ignorance inherent in that question, Rauf drew in a startled breath. 'Men and women don't usually share the facilities. But this once, we'll break with the rules and relax together.'

Good, clean, wholesome relaxation, Rauf told himself at the exact same time as he recalled how he and his friends as young boys had once fantasised about what might happen if a sexually adventurous woman were ever to enter the *hamam* when one of them was there alone. A ridiculous fantasy, for as a rule attendants were present and no such event could ever have taken place. But even so, at that point, his golden eyes flared and zeroed in on Lily's prone length of their own seeming volition. Tiny beads of perspiration already mantled the satin stretch of delicate skin below her throat. Where his libido was concerned, even looking at Lily was a mistake and all the effects of the cold dip he had enjoyed minutes earlier evaporated fast.

With a stifled groan, Rauf flipped over onto his stomach and endeavoured to control an imagination that for all his maturity was outrageously keen to zoom to the forbidden heights of male fantasy. Served him bloody well right, he told himself as his aroused sex ached with the hunger she stirred in him with such ease. Lily had said he was always totally wrapped up in himself and he could now be tormented by the knowledge that, while telling himself he only wanted to take her thoughts off the distress he had caused, he had for an inexcusable instant considered an erotic bout of passion in the *hamam* as a cure. A cure for what or whom? Where was his respect?

Lily turned over and stretched out uncertain fingers to touch his. 'You're very quiet.'

'I am only hot.' Making that charged admission, Rauf barely lifted his proud dark head.

His own family would be ashamed of him. That he had treated an innocent young woman, who had once loved him, as though she were one of the many practised lovers who had slept with him to sate a desire as basic and fleeting as his own. Lily was different. Lily had always been different, yet he knew that even three years ago he had fought that truth with every fibre of his being.

Disturbed by his tension, Lily sat up and whispered worriedly, 'You do believe what I told you about Brett?'

'Yes,' Rauf ground out, struggling to achieve mastery over a wild tide of imaginative excesses and concentrate on less dangerous and more important issues.

Shifting to within inches of him, Lily studied him and tingled. His sleek brown back was taut with male power and muscle and the smooth, powerful expanse glistened with moisture. A wicked pulse stirred at the heart of her and she pressed her thighs together in mortified acknowledgement of the fierce hold he had on both her heart and her body and rested back down again by his side. In the rushing atmospheric silence, only broken by the soft sound of running water, she snatched in a shaken breath for already her breasts felt languorous and heavy, the tender buds stiff and sensitive. He had taught her to want him and now the wanting came on its own and she could not control it.

'Maybe I should go back to bed...' Lily muttered shamefacedly.

Rauf glanced across at her, shimmering golden eyes encountering hers and reading a guilty longing there that smashed his own self-command. In the space of a moment, he reacted with all the fire of his passionate temperament. One hand closing into her tumbled hair, he brought his mouth crashing down on hers with a fierce, driving hunger that made her gasp in surprise and then in helpless pleasure.

'I can't resist you...I look at you and I burn,' Rauf breathed thickly, his desire for her a fiery blaze in his possessive gaze.

Her heart hammered as lean brown fingers flicked loose the end of the towel she had tucked in and spread the two sides apart to bare her body for his appreciation. Quivering, Lily watched his heated gaze drop to the wanton sight of her straining nipples, and then he ran his tongue over the prominent buds at the same time as he stroked apart her thighs and touched her where she was so very desperate to be touched.

Excitement took her in a wave of such blinding intensity that she was lost from that instant on. He spread her out like a willing sacrifice for his enjoyment and worked his erotic way down over her shivering, gasping length until the only awareness she possessed centred on the incredible heights of sensation her own body was capable of reaching. No, she could never have guessed that anything could be as powerful as her own total absorption in what he could make her feel. When a shattering climax gripped her and hurled her even higher, she could only moan and cling to him in ecstasy, only afterwards realising in extreme embarrassment and confusion that she had reached that ultimate height without his having made love to her and that, indeed, all the pleasure had been hers and none of it his.

'Why...? I mean—?' Lily began to mumble as she grabbed frantically at the towel beneath her, desperate for its concealment.

Holding her close, Rauf smoothed her hair back from her damp brow with an unsteady hand. 'I couldn't protect you...I won't risk getting you pregnant,' he admitted in a ragged undertone, for even her bewilderment at his restraint was more than his conscience could stand at that instant. 'Go back to my room and sleep, *güzelim*. Later, we'll talk.'

At that reference to pregnancy Lily tensed, realising with dismay that she ought to have had sufficient common sense to have foreseen that danger for herself. Pulling the towel round herself with hands that were all fingers and thumbs, she slid off the platform onto limbs that were still weak as water and hurried back into the changing room without looking back. He made her feel like a wanton. He made her realise that she had not known herself until he had shown her what passion was.

Lean, strong face grim with the gravity of thoughts that he could no longer avoid, Rauf plunged into the icy pool. From the very outset of Lily's arrival in his country, he saw that he had been selfish, in fact reckless in his treatment of her. He had brought her to Sonngul, taken her to his own bed and within a very little while, for gossip was the very food of life to his people, half the neighbourhood would be scandalised by that news. The standards of moral behaviour that prevailed in the countryside were very much higher than those of the slick city society in which he moved and he had no excuse to offer on his own behalf. Were word of the intimacy of his relationship with Lily to reach the ears of the army officer, Talip Hajjar, the older man's belief in her respectability would sink without trace.

Rauf squared his broad shoulders and swung back out of the pool. The anger of the past had powered his initial aggressive attitude and the strength of his hunger for her had led him on to a dishonourable path before he had even registered the danger and the wrong of what he'd been doing. There was only one way in which he could make appropriate amends and protect Lily: he would marry her. With as much haste and secrecy as his wealth could buy him, he would get a wedding ring on her finger before any damage could be done to her reputation. She deserved his respect and the protection of his name.

CHAPTER SEVEN

ALTHOUGH Lily had not believed that she could sleep again, the minute her head touched the pillow she sank into a deep slumber. She wakened when a maid entered bearing a laden tray and was startled to realise that it was almost two in the afternoon; the snatched and broken hours of rest she had suffered since her arrival in Turkey had finally taken their toll.

Even as she ate, all she could think about was Rauf. Everything had happened so incredibly fast and hadn't she encouraged that? Hadn't she been ready to do almost anything to get a second chance with Rauf? Her troubled face flamed with guilty colour. She remembered her total absorption in Rauf at dawn, the shameless speed with which she had succumbed to her own passionate need for him and abandoned all control. For a lowering instant, she wondered how he had transformed her into a wanton creature without apparent self-will.

But then wasn't that her old insecurity and lack of self-esteem creeping back up out of her subconscious again? For the very first time, Lily told herself, she had reached out and taken what she wanted and she had wanted Rauf. She had always wanted Rauf. Acknowledging that, she was proud that she had found the courage that she had once lacked. She felt alive again and it had been too long since she had felt like that. When had she last been so happy? That summer with Rauf three years back. For Lily, that single fact outweighed all else for simple happiness had been in too short a supply throughout her life.

When she heard the noisy clickety-clack of a helicopter coming in low to land, she was putting on a grey short-sleeved cotton dress that Hilary had loaned her and she hurried over to the window to push back the shutter. From there, she watched Rauf spring out of the craft and stride towards the house. Just looking at the arrogant angle of his dark head, the hard, masculine perfection of his bold profile and the lithe power and command of his tall, well-built frame made her heart leap.

Rauf had had an exceptionally busy morning. He had embarked on the arrangements for a civil wedding in a remote mountain town where his name was unlikely to be recognised and where nothing any journalist might consider worthy of note appeared ever to have happened. He had then flown over to the former mining village to meet with the builders ripped off by Brett Gilman. Over a very long, typically Turkish male-bonding session, he had contrived to dissuade them from dropping the charges against Gilman. He was justly proud that he had achieved that feat without offending their need to demonstrate gratitude for the compensation he had paid.

He stopped with deliberate intent to chat to Irmak, his middle-aged and devout housekeeper, who had been most noticeable by the low profile she had embraced since Lily's arrival at Sonngul. Asking where Lily was, he referred to her as his wife while affecting not to notice the surprise, excitement and sheer relief that Irmak was incapable of concealing from him. Although he hated to tell an untruth, he already thought of Lily as his wife and, when it came to protecting her and redressing the damage he had done, he could not regret it.

Rauf strode up the stairs into the *basoda* and saw Lily, her lovely face warm with self-conscious colour, rising from the window-seat in the far corner to greet him. In one glance, he took in her ill-fitting drab dress that even his great-grandmother would have been challenged to admire and knew that his first gift to Lily when she became his wife would be a new wardrobe.

'I slept for absolutely ages,' Lily remarked in a stilted rush, assailed by a tide of discomfiture as she recalled her own abandoned response to his expertise in the *hamam*.

'I had some business to take care of,' Rauf drawled, catching her slim, restive hands in the gentle hold of his to draw her forward.

As Lily tilted her head back to look up into his dark golden gaze, familiar butterflies broke loose in her tummy, followed by a coiling twist of wicked heat that made her breath catch in her throat. She wanted that hard, handsome mouth on her own so badly she could almost taste it, almost taste *him*. A wanton little frisson of pure, helpless longing slivered through her taut figure.

'No, we're not heading back to bed, *güzelim*,' Rauf murmured in rueful reproach as if she had spoken that invitation out loud. Pressing her back down onto the divan behind her, he withdrew a step. 'Yesterday you asked me if I was in the habit of rushing into sudden passionate encounters with women and I said, "Not since I was a teenager"…an answer that should have given me pause for serious thought.'

'I don't understand…' As Rauf released her hand, a chill of fear spread through Lily's tense body. Was he saying that making love to her had been a mistake? A mistake he regretted and did not intend to repeat?

'Here in my home land, women may be the equal of men in law but if a woman embraces sexual freedom, she will lose her good name,' Rauf admitted, assessing her pale set face and lowered eyes with concern. 'If I keep you here at Sonngul, if we continue as we have begun, you will be regarded as my mistress and, no matter what happens in the future, your reputation will be irreparably damaged.'

His mistress. It had a sexy, adventurous sound to it, Lily conceded with a certain amount of pride in that designation. She loved him. Her bland workaday world had been transformed into one of colour, passion, sunlight and emotion. She did not regret sharing his bed. If she could be with him, she told herself that she did not care either what label people might put on her.

'I understand…' Lily focused with self-conscious care on the gorgeous rug on the floor. 'That's not a problem.'

Thrown by that unforeseen response, Rauf settled incredulous and startled golden eyes on her down-bent head. 'It's *not*?'

Emerging from her sybaritic vision of being Rauf's mistress and lolling about like Cleopatra on imaginary satin couches, Lily came back down to earth with a bump the minute she thought about how her sister would react to that same label. Hilary would be outraged if Lily accepted that kind of role in Rauf's life. But if that was all that was on offer, how would walking away from the guy she loved benefit her? With the conviction that she was abiding by the principles that she had already compromised but ultimately done the right thing? At that moment, that did not seem much of a consolation prize for surrendering the wonder of being with Rauf.

'Actually, being a mistress is something I'd have to think over…very carefully,' Lily admitted in a strained conclusion, cringing at an all-too-real image of Hilary coming all the way to Turkey just to give Rauf, who was not her favourite person, a piece of her mind.

'Or we could go for the alternative option,' Rauf countered, vibrant amusement brimming in his eyes before he veiled them in haste and reminded himself never, ever again to consider accepting Lily's first answer to a thought-provoking question. 'We could pay the price for being impulsive and indiscreet and just get married.'

Blue eyes widening to their fullest extent, Lily lifted her golden head and stared at him in thunderstruck amazement.

'A choice we have to make right now, I'm afraid.' Lean, powerful face taut, Rauf compressed his wide, passionate mouth. 'My family could never accept a woman who has lived openly with me as my bride. I owe both them...*and* you more respect than I have so far shown.'

Slowly, Lily began breathing again. 'You're serious about this. But I can't believe it. I can't believe you're suggesting that we marry just because we've...well, you know—'

'I know very well. I still desire you more than any other woman I have ever met, *güzelim*.'

Her eyes shone overbright and she screened them, her throat aching. 'But that's not enough, is it? Especially not for someone like you who's always hated the very idea of getting married.'

That was the moment when Rauf appreciated that he had expected Lily to accept his proposal practically before he finished speaking. Was he really that arrogant? Faint colour darkened his superb cheekbones as he braced himself to find persuasive arguments when he had already given her the only reason he considered important and it was simple, straightforward and sensible: he wanted her within reach twenty-four hours a day.

'People change.'

'But you said you would *never* change,' Lily reminded him helplessly.

Rauf spread lean, impatient hands wide. 'You shouldn't

believe everything you're told. That was three years ago. I can now see many ways in which a wife would be useful to me—'

'Useful…' Lily studied his lean, devastatingly handsome features with a sinking heart.

'I own three homes here in Turkey, an apartment in New York and another in London. A wife could take charge of them and be my hostess when I entertain…and eventually I believe I would like a child.' It was an ambition that had never before occurred to Rauf and when those words emerged from him of their own apparent volition he was as taken aback as she was.

'Honestly?' Lily gave him what could only be described as a misty-eyed look of mingled surprise and hope.

Recognising that, while she had seemed seriously underwhelmed by the amount of property he owned, that reference to his own previously unsuspected desire to multiply had struck a pure-gold chord with her, Rauf did not hesitate. 'Honestly,' he confirmed. 'So, how will you answer me now?'

'I'd like about four,' Lily confided abstractedly, fighting to keep her head out of the clouds, thinking that she could settle for caring and affection and children without too much difficulty. All right, he wasn't offering love. It wasn't the whole fairy-tale fantasy she might once have cherished in her secret dreams, but if Rauf wanted to marry her she was not about to turn him down.

Rauf expelled his breath in a startled hiss. 'Four?'

'Two?' Lily bargained, recognising that she had been too frank, too soon.

'We'll think that over. I should tell you that I've already made a preliminary booking for us to be married in a civil ceremony tomorrow afternoon.'

'Tomorrow?' Lily gasped, while noting that he had had

the assurance to go ahead and embark on those arrangements before he had even mentioned marriage to her. However, taking into account his prior aversion to connubial bliss, she was much inclined to believe that a demonstration of such enthusiasm was encouraging and ought to be rewarded rather than censured.

'I intend to allow it to be assumed that we married before we even arrived at Sonngul. In that scenario, we then stole a couple of days alone here together before we could bring ourselves to share our good news with the outside world,' Rauf imparted very drily. 'My family will be so delighted that I've finally found a bride, I don't envisage awkward questions on that score. You will be received by my relatives as if you are the Eighth Wonder of the World. Throw in the news that you want four children and a red carpet will be rolled out from here to Istanbul.'

Lily blushed and then just laughed. 'Tomorrow...' she repeated afresh, still not knowing whether she was on her head or her heels. 'What will I wear?'

'Nothing likely to attract too much attention to us,' Rauf advised.

Obviously even a hint of bridal apparel would be way out of line. Her shoulders drooped a little. 'Do we have to get married as if we're the SAS on a covert operation?'

'If we don't want to publish the fact that we have been intimate without that legal tie in place...*yes*.' Rauf dealt her troubled expression a grim look of acknowledgement. 'It's my fault that it has to be that way, but once tomorrow is over we can put this unfortunate beginning behind us.'

'When I tell Hilary about this, she'll think I've gone crazy.' Lily sighed in a daze.

'As your husband, I'll be able to sort out the mess Gilman left in his wake without too much argument from your family,' Rauf contended with satisfaction.

'As sons-in-law go, I expect you qualify as quite a catch,' Lily mused with a dizzy smile as she studied him. He was drop-dead gorgeous and he was going to be hers *for ever*. She wanted to dance round the room, do mad, silly, childish things. Wow, she was getting married. Wow, was this really happening to her? Ought she to be worrying about the reality that he was behaving out of character? She worried at her lower lip, conscience stirring. This was a once very cautious, very clever and very grounded guy suddenly acting in a very impetuous way.

'Are you feeling OK?' Lily prompted grudgingly.

'Why wouldn't I be? By the way, I need your passport to fill out the forms I obtained this morning,' Rauf responded, his thoughts clearly on more practical matters. 'A copy of your birth certificate would be even more welcome.'

'I brought a copy in case I lost my passport.' Lily rifled her bag for both items.

'Excellent. You will also need a brief medical examination before the ceremony can go ahead. I have organised that with a female doctor in the same town,' Rauf explained. 'I've already had my own check.'

Lily accompanied him into a charming sun-dappled room lined with bookshelves that nonetheless rejoiced in all the high-tech equipment of an office. 'How soon do you expect to find out anything about that bank account in London?'

Rauf sent her a keen glance. 'Why?'

'Because once that's sorted out, I assume I can then tell my sister what her ex-husband has been up to,' Lily muttered ruefully, watching a frownline draw his winged ebony brows together. 'Rauf…Hilary mightn't have been expecting to hear from me immediately, but if I don't get in touch soon she'll start worrying. I could just send her a text message on my mobile…what about that?'

Rauf stilled. 'You have a mobile phone with you?'

'Yes…'

'So great was my distrust that, had I known of its existence yesterday, I would have taken it from you,' Rauf admitted. 'I hope to get the information I requested within the next forty-eight hours. Text your sister and tell her that you're fine. When I've got all the facts, we'll fly over to England together and break the bad news and the good news face to face.'

'It would be much better that way…' Touched to the heart by that thoughtful suggestion, Lily gave him a luminous smile.

Like a male drawn by a spell of enchantment, Rauf leant down and let his sensual mouth come down with sweet, drugging intensity on hers. As she trembled and leant into him for support, her body thrumming with eagerness, Rauf loosed an earthy groan of frustration low in his throat and thrust her back from him again. Brilliant eyes ablaze with hunger, he snatched in a ragged breath.

'Tonight I sleep down here…from here on in, we're respecting the conventions—'

'But if you're planning to pretend that we were married anyway…' Lily heard herself mutter and then she flushed crimson.

'But we know we're *not*…' Lean, strong face set with stubborn determination, Rauf swept up her passport and birth certificate and began to fill out the forms he had mentioned.

He had turned her into a shameless hussy at breathtaking speed, Lily acknowledged when she later lay in solitary state in his bed, so happy and excited that she couldn't sleep.

*   *   *

At three the following afternoon, Lily fingered the intricate new wedding band adorning her finger, breathed in the heady scent of the glorious bouquet of white lilies that Rauf had given her and joined him in thanking the government official who had presided over the ceremony.

'What did he say?' Lily pressed for a translation of the older man's response as Rauf guided her back out to the sunny, deserted town square where a car waited to ferry them back to the helicopter.

'That without a doubt you are the most beautiful bride ever to grace his humble office.' Angling a look of unashamed admiration over her, Rauf swung into the car beside her. In her simple straw sun-hat and pale pink dress, she was a perfect vision and he closed his hand with possessive pride over hers.

Back at Sonngul, they dined in the arbour and lingered over the coffee. Finally Rauf went off to call his family and make his announcement about their marriage. 'I'll just tell my father. He can break the news to the rest of the family.'

After relaxing in the shade a little while longer, Lily heard a funny little tune play and sat for a few seconds wondering what it was before it dawned on her that it had to be her mobile phone.

Retrieving the phone in haste, she stabbed the answer button.

'It's Brett…'

At the sound of that eerily familiar voice, Lily sat bolt upright in her cushioned chair, goose-flesh prickling at the nape of her neck. '*Brett?* What do you want?'

In the act of walking back outdoors, having made his brief call, Rauf heard Lily speak Brett's name and initial surprise stilled him in the hallway.

'What are you doing over in Turkey?' Brett demanded rawly.

Cold with the fear that Hilary's ex-husband had always inspired in her, Lily drew in a steadying breath. As she thought of the thieving, lying and cheating Brett had utilised to rob her family blind, angry, bitter disgust overcame that fear. But on the very brink of lambasting Brett for his lack of conscience, Lily froze on the recollection that Rauf did not want Brett to be warned that his criminal activities had been exposed.

'If you're trying to make trouble for me again or sticking your nose in where it's not welcome, you're going to *pay* for it!' Brett bit out nastily.

Lily felt sick: she couldn't help it. 'I have no idea why you should talk like that,' she muttered unsteadily. 'I'm just checking out the tourist trail over here for Hilary—'

'Don't lie to me...'

'Rauf and I have just got married,' Lily heard herself say and she winced at her own cowardice for even as she spoke she knew she was throwing up Rauf like a defensive barrier, hoping that Brett would be intimidated by that news.

'Married?' Brett questioned in audible disbelief.

'*Yes*...married, so just leave me alone!' Lily told him fiercely. 'You can't threaten me now and I want nothing more to do with you—'

'Kasabian has married you...well, fancy that!' Suddenly, Brett laughed as if she had cracked the best joke of the year. 'Oh, what a wonderful world it is and oh, what grief there is going to be if the bridegroom goes digging!'

'What are you talking about?' Lily exclaimed in angry apprehension, wholly disconcerted by that facetious response.

'When the balloon goes up, you had better protect me

because if you don't that marriage of yours might just end up in the dustbin too. See you soon, Lily!' As Brett rang off Lily was left clutching the phone and staring into space.

See you soon? Her flesh crawled at that concluding threat. Surely Brett could not mean that he was actually in Turkey? She checked where his call had come from and was relieved to be able to verify from the number that he had phoned her from England. Brett had only been trying to scare her. Common sense suggested that the very last place Brett would want to visit would be the scene of his own crimes. But *what* balloon was he expecting to go up? The villas he had never built? Or the likely scam that Rauf suspected over that misnamed bank account? But why on earth would Brett think that she would protect him? For the sake of her own family? For the sake of appearances? Well, this time around, Brett had no hope, Lily thought angrily. Never again and no matter what the cost would she allow herself to go in fear of Brett's threats.

Shattered by the revealing dialogue he had just over-heard, Rauf hauled in a jagged, shuddering breath. Swing-ing away, caution making him resist the instinctive need to immediately confront Lily, he headed for the sweeping staircase instead. Just when he had finally mastered any urge to doubt Lily's veracity, he had found out the truth and, ironically, from her own lips. It was in itself suspect that Brett should contact Lily. Why, after such a bitter divorce, would he phone his ex-wife's little sister unless they had had a relationship that went beyond the usual boundaries? And why would he call at all when Lily her-self loudly professed to hate him?

Leave me alone! You can't threaten me now and I want nothing more to do with you! At some stage, Lily must've been in love with Brett Gilman. And why not? Gilman was a good five years younger than his ex-wife, blond and boyish, a lightweight charmer, but still the type a lot of women went for. Lily might not have slept with her sister's husband, but evidently Gilman had been well aware of Lily's feelings for him, might even have encouraged them and had no doubt tried to use her to his own advantage. Perhaps guilt had brought Lily to her senses, perhaps she had even wanted to confess all to her sister. Had Gilman then threatened to tell his wife that Lily had been trying to tempt him into an affair?

As Rauf reached the top of the stairs Irmak brought him a phone and he answered it. It was his mother, Seren, and she was very, very excited, having only just heard from his father that her son had got married. Rauf said not a word while his mother implied that civil marriage ceremonies were only for heathens and announced that he had to bring Lily straight home to Istanbul so that they could enjoy a *proper* family wedding.

His grandmother came on the line next and pointed out that, since he had already made his poor family wait half their lives for him to find a bride, he really had to do the deed the traditional way and in style. Rauf again said nothing for it would have been a very great challenge to get a word in edgeways.

At that point, his great-grandmother, Nelispah, took her turn on the phone. First she told him how overjoyed she was before reminiscing at some length about how her own wedding celebrations had lasted forty days and forty nights. But she then let a little sob escape as she pointed out how shocked everybody would be when they learnt that her great-grandson had wed his bride without his own family present. Of course, the simple way out of that painfully embarrassing predicament, Nelispah added in a pathetic whisper, would be to stage another wedding and act as if the civil ceremony had never happened.

'Whatever you want, anything…' Rauf muttered, barely able to keep what he was hearing in his head for longer than five seconds but aware that even more guilt was hovering heavily on his horizon.

'Are you well?' Nelispah Kasabian trilled in a more lively tone.

'I'm fine.' Rauf breathed in deep and knew he was lying.

'Bring Lily home to us tomorrow and we will see to everything,' the old lady told him chirpily and the call ended much faster than he would have expected it to end, but as it was a relief at that instant he brushed aside his faint surprise.

Rauf's next conscious move was in the direction of the drinks cabinet. The phone call was already forgotten. He poured himself a brandy. He couldn't keep his hand steady and the rage of shock was now coursing through him like molten lava. But what was he planning to say to Lily? Indeed could he even reasonably say anything?

For, three years ago, he himself had come a poor second-best to Brett Gilman! He broke out in a cold sweat at that humiliating acknowledgement. But it was obvious. Everything in his past relationship with Lily that had once puzzled Rauf now fell into place: her former aversion to being touched by him, her surprising reluctance to visit her own family. When he had first met Lily in London, she could only have been trying to get over her love for her sister's husband and dating Rauf had most likely been part of that effort.

In those days, Lily had neither wanted nor needed nor loved him. She might have recently said that she *had* loved him then, but he saw that as a case of wishful thinking, a case of wanting to forget an attachment that still made her feel guilty. How could she ever have loved him when it was so evident that it had been Brett she still cared about? However, Lily did want him *now*, Rauf reminded himself doggedly. But did she still languish after Gilman in some secret corner of her heart? The fact that she had broken off the relationship didn't mean that she had stopped loving the guy, didn't mean that she wouldn't still try to save his useless hide if she got the chance! Since time immemorial supposedly sane women had been falling in love with hardened criminals they longed to redeem.

Furthermore, Lily would not be impressed if he killed Gilman with his bare hands because, right then, Rauf felt more than equal to doing that. Dead competition had a lot less pulling power. After all, how would Lily react when Gilman went to prison? Rauf expelled his pent-up breath in a shaken surge for he felt as if he were coming apart at the seams with not a shade of his rational intellect left intact. But Lily was *his*, wasn't she? No other man, nothing was about to get in the way of that reality. He was not going to lose her. Lily was his wife. Possession would be ten tenths of the law in his household.

He embarked on a second brandy. He would say nothing…he *could* say nothing! Falling in love with the wrong person was not a crime. Indeed, it seemed clear that Lily had behaved exactly as she ought to have done in the circumstances: there had been no affair. She had left home, stayed away and resisted temptation. He ought to be proud of her for that, Rauf told himself fiercely. But that was a step too far for him at that moment. He was still too devastated by what he had learned.

Pale and taut, Lily went off in search of Rauf. He was in the *basoda*, his back turned to the room as he stared out the window. Even in the state she was in, she noted the rigidity of his stance, the bunched muscles evident in his wide shoulders as he flexed them in a sudden abrupt movement that lacked his usual fluid grace.

'I suppose your family was sure to be upset about you marrying a woman they've never met…' Lily sighed unhappily, assuming that that was why he had not returned to the arbour.

Rauf closed his eyes for a second and then swung round, dark eyes veiled. 'No…nothing of that nature and you did meet my great-grandmother briefly,' he reminded her.

'They probably think you've made the biggest mistake of your life…just suddenly plunging into marriage with a stranger,' Lily suggested next, determined to know the worst.

Conscious that she was staring at him, Rauf made a major effort to concentrate. 'I told my father that we first met a few years ago. It was the fact that we opted for a civil ceremony and went ahead without their presence which caused some distress…I think—'

Her brow indented. 'You…*think*?'

His beautifully shaped brows knit. 'I believe I may have promised to take you to Istanbul tomorrow.'

'Oh…' Lily worried at her lower lip and then pressed ahead. 'I've something I have to tell you. Brett just called me on my mobile phone.'

Impressed by that honesty, Rauf studied her with dark eyes beginning to flare gold.

'I didn't let him know you were on to him!' Lily hurried to reassure him. 'He takes my nieces out on Friday evenings—well, at least he's *supposed* to, but most weeks he doesn't turn up—only presumably he did show yesterday and I bet one of the girls mentioned that I was over here. I suspect that that must have put Brett in a panic…so I said I was just here doing the tourist trail for Hilary…I also mentioned us being married…'

At the very top of her voice, Rauf recalled, striding forward to gather her straight in his arms. In the midst of wondering why Rauf had made no comment whatsoever about Brett's call, Lily was engulfed in an embrace so passionate that every powerful, angular line of his hard, muscular physique imprinted on her softer, more yielding curves. His tongue slid between her lips and plundered the tender interior of her mouth until she shivered against him, buried her hands in his thick black hair and surrendered to being lifted right off her feet.

'It's OK for you to make a habit of this…' Lily mumbled through reddened lips as he carried her off towards their bedroom. 'In fact, I rather like it.'

A vague recollection of Brett's call slid back into her mind. 'Aren't you annoyed about Brett phoning me?' she asked abstractedly.

'Not at all…obvious move for him to make.' Rauf contrived to answer with only the very faintest edge in his rich, dark drawl. 'But let's not talk about him on our wedding night, *güzelim*.'

'Wedding evening,' Lily whispered, feeling truly wicked and loving it and so grateful he wasn't one whit bothered about Brett having called.

CHAPTER EIGHT

SETTING her down beside the bed, Rauf removed Lily's sun-hat and embarked on the dozen hairgrips she had used to pile most of her glorious mane up out of sight.

Blue eyes bright as jewels, she looked up at him. 'I'm really happy,' she told him.

Who was she keenest to convince? Herself? Rauf shut down on that thought as soon as it surfaced but it led right on in to another. Right now, was she trying not to think about Brett? Of course, she was! How could she not be thinking of the bastard after he had just phoned her? He *had* to get rid of that phone. What had happened once was not going to happen a second time.

Recognising the aggressive thrust of his jawline, troubled by his unusual silence, Lily whispered worriedly, 'Do you have regrets about marrying me already?'

'Are you crazy?' Rauf launched at her with a force of instant rebuttal that struck her as a not quite convincing overreaction.

'It's all right to admit it…I'd sooner know…we did go into this a bit fast,' Lily conceded tightly.

'I can't imagine my life without you,' Rauf breathed tautly.

'But I've only been back in your life four days…'

'Four days is long enough with a lifetime ahead of us,' Rauf swore, backing off a step to throw off his jacket and wrench at his silk tie. 'My great-grandfather asked for Nelispah's hand in marriage the first day he saw her…'

'Love at first sight.' Lily was impressed.

'Or the fact that the men in her family said he was a dead man if he *didn't* marry her,' Rauf traded with sudden grudging amusement.

'I don't believe you…'

'You should. He was on a walking tour of the mountain villages. Quite by accident he saw Nelispah bathing in a river in her underwear and she liked the look of him so she told her brothers about it. Her brothers liked the look of him too because a Turk prosperous enough to take a holiday seventy-five years ago was a rich man on their terms. So forty days later he came back down the mountain with a wife and *said* it was love at first sight—'

Lily was fascinated. 'Why forty days later?'

'Village weddings used to be extremely lengthy affairs.'

'And your grandmother…how did she meet your grandfather?'

'With a great deal of cunning because in those days only parents arranged marriages and daughters were never allowed out without a chaperone. She dropped her scarf in the street, he picked it up and then it was the love-at-firstsight story all over again,' Rauf delivered cynically. 'My parents were the same. They got one glimpse of each other at a wedding and my mother went into a decline until my grandfather agreed to her marrying him…at the time he wanted her to marry someone else.'

'You have a very romantic family tree.' Lily tried not to say what was on her mind but in the end could not hold her curiosity in. 'So why did you have to be different?'

'Because the girl I thought I loved at nineteen was in love with one of my best friends…but she would *still* have married me because I was a richer catch.' The minute he'd said it, Rauf admitted that he was irritated with himself, for even his family had no idea how close he had come then to fulfilling their fondest hopes.

'Oh, no…that must have been awful for you,' Lily exclaimed with the kind of ready sympathy that made him grit his teeth. 'How did you find out?'

'I found them rolling about a bed at a party.' Rauf shrugged with expressive finality and went back to unbuttoning his shirt. 'It was no big deal. I got over it. Don't get the idea that I went off marriage because of that one bad experience.'

'Of course not…' Lily swallowed hard but she could imagine how vulnerable he must have been as a teenager, especially after having been raised on a careful diet of romantic love-at-first-sight stories by his shrewd but over-protective family. 'Was she one of the girls your relatives were hoping you would marry?'

'Yes. How the hell did we get onto this subject?' Rauf demanded.

Lily did something she had never done before. Seeing that a distraction was called for, she reached behind herself and undid the zip on her dress. Then she let the sleeves drift down her extended arms and the entire garment finally dropped in a heap round her toes.

The strangest ache stirred in Rauf's chest. He couldn't understand why he didn't laugh when she shimmied out of her dress with that taut, flushed air of daring and stood there revealed *in*…a full-length white cotton petticoat that revealed very little more than the dress had. 'Love the frills,' he breathed huskily.

Lily had forgotten she was wearing the petticoat. 'That dress is a bit see-through,' she muttered awkwardly.

'I wouldn't have liked that at all,' Rauf asserted instantly, moving fluidly forward to spin her round and peel her out of the petticoat.

Lily shut her eyes tight and leant forward as he let his mouth drift down the exposed line of her spine and a faint moan parted her lips. He caught her back against him, the shirt he still wore falling open to bring the smooth skin of her back into contact with the hard muscularity of his hair-roughened chest. As she quivered he whispered, 'Want me?'

'Can't help it...' Lily admitted.

'That's how it should be.' *But how much did she want him?* a little demon in Rauf's conscious mind taunted. Enough to turn down Gilman had circumstances been different? If she was content to settle for sex and look for nothing more, wasn't that his *own* fault?

'Exactly as it should be.' Rauf breathed in deep to continue with a roughened sexy edge to his drawl that made Lily's toes curl. Unclipping her bra, he let it fall and his hands curved round to mould the creamy swell of her breasts. 'You're my wife.'

A long, sighing gasp broke from her as he toyed with her taut rose-tipped nipples. A little flame had already flickered into a slow burn low in her belly. She squeezed her eyes tight shut in shame because she couldn't keep herself still, couldn't prevent her hips from squirming back into connection with the bold thrust of his arousal, couldn't think of anything but the pleasure to come.

He nipped at a tiny pulse point below her ear with his teeth and she jerked, already well on the way to meltdown. Not a sound did she make as he caught her up in his arms and tumbled her down on the bed.

'Look at me,' Rauf commanded.

Lily opened dazed eyes feeling as if she had 'wanton' stamped all over her. Her total inability to do anything but revel in his every caress still seemed vaguely indecent to her.

'What are you thinking about?'

'You…' A wave of colour washed her fair complexion. 'What you do to me.'

A brilliant smile flashed across his mouth and she rested back limp with incredible longing and love. He discarded his shirt. She watched his every move from below the screen of her lashes, breath catching in her throat at his sleek male beauty, heart thumping a little faster each time.

'You didn't use to think of me like that…' Rauf said thickly.

'I *did*…' As he gave her a disbelieving look, Lily came up on one elbow, struggling to find the right words to explain. 'It's just when I tried to make the…dream real, I…I couldn't…'

And why had that been? Because Gilman had had her loyalty and her love, Rauf reflected with vicious anger, swinging away with scorching golden eyes to toss his Rolex watch down on the cabinet.

'But I can now,' Lily muttered, noticing the hard set of his masculine profile, feeling the dangerous vibes emanating from his lean, powerful frame, trying to understand what she had said that had had that effect.

'I'll make every dream real,' Rauf intoned as though she had thrown down a gauntlet.

'You already do…' Lily confided half under her breath, absorbed in the insidiously sexy way he stripped off his trousers, noting the way the light coming through the window glistened over the fine furrow of dark hair running down over his hard, flat stomach. As the boxer shorts came off her eyes widened and she blushed for herself. The tiny beat of need already pulsing at the very centre of her throbbed.

'You make me so hot…' Rauf confessed, coming down on the bed with all the easy grace of a prowling tiger, plundering her reddened lips and letting his tongue delve deep in a darting, erotic imitation of a more intimate penetration.

The meltdown point came back to Lily fast. She just looked at him and dizzy joy grabbed hold of her because, now that they were married, she felt that he was finally hers and that emotional high of loving heightened her every response. He stroked the sensitive pink tips of her breasts, employed his knowing mouth there, shaped her tender flesh, worked his expert path down over her slender, gasping body, discovering pulse points she had not known existed and lingering there with a quite devastating effect on her self-control.

'I want this to be superlative,' Rauf muttered fiercely when she was way beyond grasping words of more than two syllables with any degree of comprehension.

She tried to touch him, she was desperate to touch him, smooth worshipping hands over the sleek, tight skin of his muscles, discover the solid wall of his chest with her palms and let her own lips explore and taste him as he tasted her. But every time she got anywhere near to fulfilling that need he pinned her back flat to the bed and overwhelmed her with more sensation. She was panting for breath, half out of her mind with excitement, her hips writhing long before he deigned to seek out the damp, aching heat at the heart of her.

'Rauf...' she moaned.

'Don't be so impatient,' he husked.

And somewhere around then, all sense of time and place left Lily. She didn't know what was happening any more. The excitement would build and build and then he would let it fall again until she wanted to scream and almost did. It was like being tortured with pleasure and her body was driven from one excruciating high of frustration to the next.

'Please…' she gasped.

'Please what…?' Rauf teased in a suggestive growl, sizzling golden eyes intent on her, enjoying his power over her.

'Don't stop…please don't stop,' she practically sobbed, begging, helpless, desperate for that unbearable need to be quenched.

He came over her and into her then, in one forceful movement and she almost passed out on the shock wave of incredible pleasure. Intense excitement took over and finally sent her flying over the edge into ecstasy and into an explosive shower of sensation that seemed to last for ever. In the aftermath, she felt drained, shell-shocked, still out of her own body, but she fought off the drowsy relaxation threatening to claim her.

Rauf rolled over and took her with him, arranging her over his hot, damp, sprawled length with a possessive intimacy that warmed her even when she was angry with him. As he closed both arms tightly round her and claimed another kiss, part of her wanted to just lie there and make appreciative noises, but another part of her wanted to kick him for his arrogant need to control her.

Golden eyes slumbrous with very male satisfaction, Rauf murmured, 'That *was*—'

'You at your most domineering…' Lily slotted in helplessly, lifting her tousled head, face hot but eyes reproachful.

Rauf laced long lazy fingers into her tumbled hair. 'So you can go for domineering in a very big way, *güzelim*,' he countered silkily.

Lily trailed herself free of him and suppressed a sigh, knowing she ought not to say what she wanted to say, knowing she was going to say it anyway because it hurt so much not to be loved. 'Maybe I wanted romantic…'

'Was Brett romantic?' Rauf asked in a tone of derision.

Lily blinked and then turned her head in confusion. 'What's he got to do with anything?'

'I was just curious,' Rauf drawled smooth as honey.

'Well, how would I know?' Lily grimaced and turned away again, thinking of the way Rauf had made love to her. Wild, inventive, exciting, full marks, she guessed, for technique, expertise. Was it such a turn off when she touched him? Was she so inept? And had he had to demonstrate his superior control with such humiliating completeness that she had ended up virtually begging for him to make love to her?

'I can do romantic...' Rauf asserted, tugging her back to him.

Lily stiffened. 'No...you can do sex.'

'Don't be crude...I don't expect that from you.'

Lily had never attracted an accusation like that in her life before. Crude?

'Sex...sex...sex...*sex*!' Lily hissed back at him like a furious spitting cat.

In a sudden movement, Rauf leant over her, propped his blue-shadowed jawline on the heel of one lean hand and studied her with wickedly amused golden eyes and a lazy, electrifying smile. 'Petticoat...petticoat...petticoat.'

The volatile speed at which Rauf could change mood had always disconcerted her. As Lily gazed up at him in chagrin he lifted her hand and threaded an exquisite diamond ring onto her finger next to her wedding ring. 'Romantic,' he pointed out.

'Where did it come from?'

'I put it under the pillow before I got into bed.'

Dumbstruck, Lily surveyed the glorious diamond cluster from all angles.

Rauf shifted with lithe masculine intent into a more intimate position over her. 'What's my score now?'

'Eleven out of ten…it's a very beautiful ring.' Lily sighed, feeling incredibly tired and knowing that she should have guessed that he would excel at one-upmanship. He loathed being criticised and it was their wedding night. It wasn't the time to tell him that, no matter how incredible he was in bed, no matter how intense her own response, having to plead for him to make love to her made her feel small.

He gave her a challenging look and then freed her to sprawl back across the pillows, all lithe indolence and gorgeous masculinity. 'But I would *hate* to be thought domineering.'

Impervious to hints and with a sleepy smile, Lily just wriggled back across the divide he had opened up between them and snuggled up to him as if he were a large teddy bear. 'I can hardly keep my eyes open,' she mumbled round a stifled yawn. 'And I don't want to look like a hag when I meet your family tomorrow.'

'You couldn't look like a hag if you tried,' Rauf groaned and tucked her under his arm.

But he then lay there smouldering and trying not to wonder if she would have gone to sleep on Brett. It was not that he was jealous or competitive, just that he was sensitive. She might be his wife but he was not about to make a fool of himself over her. So why was he staying in bed at ten in the evening wide awake but holding her tight as if she might be about to make a break for freedom? She was his wife; she wasn't going anywhere. And if she ever did, he would soon fetch her back.

All things considered, he decided that he felt remarkably good in spite of overhearing that phone call. He relaxed and listed all the physical things he liked most about her.

The smell and the feel of her hair, the smoothness of her skin, the blue of her eyes and the sparkle there when she smiled, the trusting way she curved round him. Trusting her, though, was still a challenge. He would never tell her that that diamond ring was three years old.

The next morning, Lily ended up in a mad rush. Having breakfasted in bed and promised Rauf she would only be half an hour, she went through everything in her luggage before finally settling on wearing a lilac skirt and toning shirt that looked more formal and smart than anything else she had with her. But when she emerged breathlessly from her room, she found Rauf's housekeeper waiting to intercept her in company with one of the maids who spoke English and who explained that Irmak wanted to give Lily the official guided tour of the house. Reluctant to risk causing offence, Lily smiled and just hoped that Rauf would be patient.

She loved Sonngul. It was a timeless, special place where she and Rauf had found each other again without the intrusion of the outside world. She was duly admiring the tall, serried ranks of pristine bedding in the huge linen cupboard when Rauf appeared and gave her a pained masculine appraisal. 'We have to be at the airport in less than an hour...what are you looking at sheets for?'

'Irmak was pleased,' Lily chided.

As they passed the door of the room he used as an office he paused and strode in to wait for the fax that was spewing out papers. Tucking them at speed into the file lying on the desk, he lifted the file and rejoined her.

'If I hadn't had work demanding my attention, I would've stayed in bed later.' In the shaded privacy of the path that led out to the helipad, Rauf claimed a hungry kiss that made her senses sing.

At Bodrum airport, Lily could only be impressed by the

sleek private jet that bore an MMI logo on the tail fin that awaited them.

'This is definitely how to travel,' she confided after take-off, studying the big, luxurious cabin and the amount of space surrounding her cream leather seat.

There was no response from her bridegroom and she smiled. Rauf was settled by the built-in desk opposite, a laptop computer sitting open in readiness, and his entire attention appeared to be consumed by the contents of the file he had brought with him.

Rauf had not realised that one of the faxes that had arrived before he'd left Sonngul was a response from the Turkish bank he had requested information from. Therefore when he initially glanced at the sheet in the act of leafing through the file, he could not at first grasp why Lily's name was printed there. And then he saw Brett Gilman's name as well and comprehension dawned at an excessively slow speed, for Rauf did not want to believe the evidence before his eyes.

There *had* to be a mistake. He angled a sideways glance at Lily from below dense black lashes. She was watching him and she gave him a sunny smile as if she had not a care in the world.

'Lily…' Rauf breathed without any expression at all.

Something in his voice made her tense and she looked at him and connected with piercing dark eyes. 'What is it?'

Rauf rose upright in one forceful motion and stared down at her, not a muscle moving in his lean dark face. 'You must've known that I was going to find out. Is that why you married me?'

A frown line indented her brow. 'What on earth is the matter?'

Rauf lounged back against the side of the desk, raw

incredulity and rage beginning to flame inside him. He had
made it so simple for her. He could not credit his own
stupidity. She had run rings round him! Had he really believed that he was the one controlling events? In the space
of four days, she had got his wedding ring on her finger
and, with that single achievement, she had made herself
safe from all threats.

After all, it really didn't matter what he found out *now*,
did it? She could afford to sit there and look politely enquiring, for he wasn't likely to prosecute his own wife,
was he? He had married a thief. A lying, greedy little thief,
who had conspired with Brett Gilman to defraud him of
over two-hundred-thousand pounds. He snatched up the
fax he had been sent and slung it down in front of her.

Lily lifted the sheet and tried to read, only to say, 'But
this is in Turkish—'

'I'm sure you're capable of reading your own name and
Brett's,' Rauf derided.

Lily looked up at him, frightened by the dark bleakness
of his accusing gaze. 'My name and Brett's? What is this?
Where did you get it?'

'You and Gilman opened that bank account for
Marmaris Media Incorporated *together*,' Rauf spelt out so
softly that she almost strained to hear him. 'And guess
what, the little bad fairies have been in and they have
emptied the account just as I expected!'

CHAPTER NINE

LILY lost colour as she finally grasped what Rauf was talking about. 'I did not open any bank account with Brett!' she protested.

'Yes, you *did*. It's down here in black and white in this fax,' Rauf pointed out with a rawer edge to his deep, dark drawl, his fabulous bone structure rigid, his pallor below his bronzed skin pronounced.

'Well, then, someone's made a mistake...or Brett has set me up. That's the only possible explanation!' Lily flung back at him, and no longer able to bear him standing over her like a very tall building casting a menacing dark shadow, she jumped up out of her seat.

'Don't waste my time. I don't believe you. You conspired with Gilman to steal from me!'

Lily was shaking from the terrifying and frustrating awareness that she seemed to have been tried, judged and found guilty on the spot. Nor did Rauf appear to have the slightest intention of hearing a word she said in her own defence.

'That's not true. How can you even *think* that I could do such a thing?' she asked with shocked distaste. 'For goodness' sake, I'm your wife!'

Dark colour accentuated the taut angularity of Rauf's superb cheekbones and he spread both hands into a violent arc. 'Yes, you're my bride. That's quite a coup I gave you, isn't it? You must've been laughing all the way down the line at me—'

'I've had enough. I am not even going to try to talk to you in the mood you're in—'

'Oh, yes, you *are*,' Rauf bit out, closing strong hands to her wrists before she could complete her intent and drop back into her seat again. 'And I warn you…your usual, very effective ploy of turning on the waterworks won't silence me this time around!'

'At this moment, Rauf Kasabian…' as Lily wrenched her wrists free of his hold her blue eyes burned like the sapphire centre of a flame over his lean, darkly attractive features '…I wouldn't cry if you tied me to a stake and stood over me with a match!'

'At last a piece of *good* news. I also think you need to know when and where my suspicions about you and Brett began—'

'Inside your own very colourful imagination?' Lily sliced in.

Incensed by that scornful suggestion, Rauf flashed her a scorching look of pure intimidation. 'Tecer Godian…do you remember him?'

Disconcerted, Lily muttered, 'Mr Godian, your last ac-countant…the one who came over to England to check out Harris Travel three years ago?'

'Tecer was an astute man. That last day that I stayed at your home, you said you had to go into the travel agency to help out because an employee was ill. Tecer was there checking the accounts and so were you and Brett. Even though Tecer saw nothing that he could quite put his finger on, he saw enough to rouse his concern—'

'What do you mean?'

'Tecer had no idea that I was personally involved with you. Later that same morning, he said to me, ''The son-in-law, Brett…and Lily, the wife's little sister, there's something wrong and disturbing about that relationship.

They don't behave like *normal* family members do with each other.'''

At that revelation, Lily tensed with surprise. Had Tecer Godian noted her fear and nervous tension at being alone, as she had initially believed, with her brother-in-law in the front office? Her considerable relief when she had first registered that the older man was in the back room going over the accounts and her chattiness once Brett had mercifully gone out? Yes, as Rauf so rightly said, Tecer had been a shrewd man, as an outsider seeing what those more closely involved did not see. But Rauf had taken those astute warning words and put them into a very different context.

'I paid no heed, asked no questions, but I understood what Tecer meant all right after I had waited in that car park until you finally emerged from that hotel with Gilman!' Rauf grated in contemptuous condemnation. 'Even though you refuse to admit it, all along you were in love with your sister's husband—'

'That's *not* what the man saw between Brett and I,' Lily argued with furious emphasis. 'It's a pity that you never asked Tecer to explain what he meant—'

'Do you think that I would've lowered myself to the level of discussing you with a man who was not only my employee, but also a family friend?' Rauf scorned.

'You might have saved us both a lot of unhappiness if you had,' Lily condemned with angry reproach, finally understanding what had first made Rauf suspect the nature of her relationship with her sister's ex-husband. 'But perhaps you took out of his words what you *wanted* to believe—'

'And what the hell is that supposed to mean? We're straying too far from the main issue here,' Rauf condemned with brooding force, shimmering golden eyes pinned to the flushed, taut oval of her face. 'My every worst suspicion about your integrity has been proved correct.'

'And that's a relief for you, isn't it?' Lily studied him with wondering eyes, bitter anger of a strength she had never before experienced building even higher inside her. 'To believe that I loved Brett, that I only took you home so that you could invest in Harris Travel and that all the time my sole motivation was to enrich Brett and get my own greedy hands on your wretched money?'

His aggressive jawline clenched, for it infuriated him that, even when he set the evidence before her, she was *still* striving to portray herself as a poor little victim. 'Yes...that is what I must believe.'

Lily loosed a jagged little laugh. 'Then I'm sure this can't come as a surprise to you either...I very much regret getting married to you yesterday!'

'Like hell you do!' Rauf countered in a lion's roar of rebuttal that shook her where she stood. 'If you weren't my wife, I'd be handing you straight over to the police!'

'Hopefully they would be a little better at investigating crime than you are...then that's their job,' Lily traded with dulcet sweetness of tone, her powerful sense of injustice mounting as she had considered all the sins that he seemed to believe her capable of committing. 'So go ahead and hand me over because I don't ever want to have anything more to do with you!'

'Let me tell you, after a few nights in a prison cell you wouldn't be half so bloody impertinent!' Rauf launched back at her, incensed by what he interpreted as a ridiculous declaration. 'And what's more, you married me knowing that you were protecting yourself from any threat of imprisonment—'

'My goodness...' Lily trilled, burning spots of furious

colour now highlighting her cheekbones. 'I ought to write a book about my life as a wicked, unscrupulous adventuress…only I don't seem to have been a very successful one, do I?'

'What's that supposed to mean?' Rauf demanded.

'Well, according to you, I loved Brett and cheated, lied and stole for him, but somehow never had the guts to be wicked enough to sleep with him,' Lily recounted with wide, questioning eyes. 'Then there's also the small fact that I'm virtually broke until my next month's salary arrives, so I appear to have been a total loser as an embezzler as well. And, lastly, my crowning error seems to have been to marry the guy I robbed…which hardly promises me the happiest of secure futures…does it?'

His devastatingly handsome features clenched hard. 'If I receive one more facetious response from you—'

'You'll what…divorce me?' Lily slung at him bitterly. 'Well, I'm ahead of you there…*I* want a divorce!'

Rauf went rigid at that threat and instantly asserted, 'You can forget that as an option—'

'*And* you can keep your lousy money too. I'll think myself lucky just to be free from the nightmare of being tied to a guy who has no faith in me at all!'

'You're married to me and, I'm afraid, there's no escape clause in this lifetime,' Rauf heard himself launch back at her in an even blacker rage.

'I'd rather take my chances with the police…I'll hand myself over, get this sorted out,' Lily declared again, her chin taking on a defiant tilt.

'Don't be stupid!' Rauf seethed, out of all patience with her.

'I did *not* put my name on that bank account—'

'Stop *lying* to me! Gilman needed your name on the account because you're a director in Harris Travel, which means that he can lie and say he opened up that account as an employee at *your* request! As a director, you can be held liable for the disappearance of the funds I invested in the firm!'

Without warning, Lily's knees betrayed a lowering need to knock together in fright and she sank down into a seat on the other side of the cabin. She had not realised that the awarding of that directorship by her father from which she had yet to earn a single penny meant that she could be put in such a position. Now at last she understood why Brett had smugly informed her that *she* would have to protect *him*. Very probably, Brett had put her name on the account with his own for the reasons that Rauf had just defined, and no wonder her sister's ex-husband had crowed when she had announced that she and Rauf had just got married! Brett would also have foreseen the unlikelihood of Rauf choosing to press charges over the stolen cash when to do so would cast doubt on his own wife's honesty. But Lily could not abide even the idea of Brett Gilman escaping his just deserts!

Having thought that through, having cast her mind back over the misery Brett had sentenced her to suffer when she'd been too young and naive to know how to fight back, Lily breathed in slow and deep to strengthen herself. She was very pale but she folded her trembling hands together on her lap and finally lifted her head high. 'Well, it's better that I should be held liable than either my sister, who has children, or my father, who has a string of health problems,' she pointed out with quiet determination.

'When are you going to stop talking nonsense?' Rauf demanded, throwing his arms wide in incredulous roaring frustration, for the dialogue was travelling into fanciful realms that made no sense at all to him. 'There will be *no* prosecution about the missing money for the very obvious reason that I am not prepared to label my wife a thief!'

'But that would mean that Brett got off scot-free…and *I* couldn't stand that,' Lily stated. 'He has caused my family and me so much unhappiness that I want him to pay for it even if it means that I have to tolerate suspicion being cast on me for a while. But I firmly believe that the truth will come out…and that in a law court his guilt would be proved.'

Rage beginning to dwindle in the face of such agonisingly naive statements, Rauf studied Lily with the inescapable conviction that once again, against all belief and the apparent facts, he had jumped to the wrong conclusion. From where he stood, he could practically feel the flames of idealistic, self-sacrificing fervour Lily exuded and he snatched up that fax from the Turkish bank's head office with a hand that was far from steady.

Her name was on the account but that was not actual evidence that she herself had put it there. After all, what was to have prevented Gilman from taking another blonde woman into the bank to open that account and supplying a piece of identification purloined from Lily without her knowledge? Nor had she been a co-signatory on the account, which meant that the withdrawals had been made solely by Gilman. In fact, Rauf registered at that second, calmer reappraisal, Lily's name being on that account bore all the hallmarks of a clumsy attempt by Gilman to cover his own tracks and spread the blame. Suddenly, he was certain that he would discover on further investigation that Lily's signature on opening the account had been forged. Lily had reacted with honest anger and she had no fear of talking to the police. Furthermore, no *sane* guilty woman would seek to defend herself and engage his support by angrily abusing him and threatening to divorce him!

'We're going to be meeting my family in little more than an hour,' Rauf drawled not quite levelly because, so shattered was he by the belief that he had again misjudged her, clinging to what he saw as a safe certainty felt comforting. He had fallen once more into the same chasm of doubting her and he cursed the jealousy that had clouded his judgement. He knew he had to redress the damage he had done and grovel…only grovelling was not a talent that had ever come to Rauf in any shape or form.

Lily gaped at him. 'I'm hardly going to go ahead with that now—'

'But you have convinced me that you are innocent of any blame. I wasn't prepared for that fax and I overreacted to it and I must apologise to you. A more level-headed examination of the facts does indeed suggest that Gilman has tried to frame you,' Rauf asserted levelly.

'But it's obvious that you've never been able to trust me,' Lily said tightly. 'Your suspicions about Brett and I have always been there and have never gone away—'

'But it's all out in the open now and I'm finally convinced that there was *never* anything inappropriate in your dealings with Gilman!' Rauf swore with fierce intensity, dark-as-midnight eyes glittering, revealing his steadily rising stress level, for he was not accustomed to Lily not listening to what he said or rejecting his pleas in his own defence. 'Right now, I don't give a damn about him…I'm much more concerned about *us*—'

'Why would that be? Even though you couldn't trust me, you still married me. I find that very strange and extremely hurtful,' Lily confessed a little unsteadily, for tears were prickling at the back of her aching eyes. 'But that's the way it is and what it means is that you have never *cared* for me as you ought to care for me—'

'You are totally wrong about that.' Getting tenser by the

second, for Lily was in a frame of mind he had never before had to deal with, Rauf strode forward and attempted to reach for her hands. However, Lily only shrank back and coiled her fingers even tighter together, resisting even his touch.

'No, I'm not…from start to finish, all you can ever have wanted from me was sex and all you still want from me is sex…and you're *so* obsessed with the sex that you were even willing to stay married to a woman whom you once believed not only carried on with her own sister's husband, but also stole from you!' Lily condemned in tight, jerky spurts of words. 'I don't think that's healthy. I don't think anyone would think *that* was healthy—'

'And put like that it doesn't sound healthy either.' Rauf groaned with a feeling grimace, dropping down into an athletic crouch beside her seat and striving to gain eye contact because he knew that always got results. 'But to write off everything that is between us as just sex is outrageous—'

'I think so too, but then I also think you're just orientated that way,' Lily muttered ruefully, finally looking up to connect with his beautiful dark golden eyes and the rather stunned light that was starting to take root there. 'You're also the most dreadfully suspicious guy I have ever met—'

'But only over this *one* single issue,' Rauf interrupted at speed, desperate for her to make that distinction. 'And that issue is that bastard, Gilman, and every single misunderstanding that has occurred between us has related to him in some way—'

'I really don't think you can call accusing your own wife of being a thief…a misunderstanding,' Lily interrupted heavily.

'I have a very quick temper and an obvious and very

regrettable propensity for leaping to the wrong conclusion when it comes to you.' Pouncing on her hands the instant her slender fingers loosened their grip on each other, Rauf tugged her upright out of her seat. 'But that is only because I care so *much* about you. I'm sorry, *güzelim.*'

But just then even the rare sight of Rauf looking drawn and taut with strain could not make Lily swerve in her convictions. She had always loved him and as a result felt she had been much too willing to overlook the flaws in their relationship. But now harsh reality had punctured her happiness and she believed all that she had said to him. She also reckoned that he was hopeless at working out what went on inside his own complex head. After all, he had looked very shocked when she had said that his sole interest in her was sex, but when had he ever mentioned anything else?

'I'm sure you can explain to your family that you made a mistake getting married to me in such haste—'

'They'd still expect me to bring the mistake home,' Rauf cut in with helpless irony as he settled her back in her seat and did up her belt because the jet was soon to land. 'In the Kasabian family, when you get married, you *stay* married—'

'Maybe the Harris women have a fatal habit of marrying the wrong men—'

'Putting me on a level with Gilman is hitting *way* below the belt—'

'If we've already split up, it would be less embarrassing for you when I'm helping the police with their enquiries,' Lily told him flatly.

'You won't be helping the police with *any* enquiries!' Rauf countered with savage determination, his adrenalin racing at the mere mention of such a development, and at the same time as he spoke he saw his entire system of values take a metaphorical lurch into new and dangerously disturbing territory. For hadn't he too once believed that it was always right to speak the truth? Only now intelligence was suggesting the direct opposite. That fax made Lily look like an embezzler and Gilman's co-conspirator.

Just then, Rauf registered that there was *nothing* that he would not do to protect Lily from potential harm. And if protecting Lily meant lying and burying the evidence to ensure that she could in no way be tainted or threatened by Gilman's crimes, he would do it without hesitation. He was shocked by that awareness but he only had to look at Lily and think of her in a prison cell and every one of his ethics and every one of his principles went into hiding and what was left immediately assured him that the ends justified the means.

As the jet landed Lily was in a complete daze at the far-reaching decisions she had made. Yet, Brett *had* to be stopped. Enough was enough. What other awful things might Brett do if he was left free? Was she to spend the rest of her days in secret fear of the man? And why should Rauf lose his money because he had married her? That would be wrong. It would be even more wrong if Rauf or his family were to suffer embarrassment through his having married a woman in danger of being arrested for fraud. After all, if she could be held liable as a director of Harris Travel for the disappearance of Rauf's investment that also meant that she could be held liable for the villa fraud as well…didn't he realise that she saw that now?

She shivered, cold, quaking dismay springing her from her daze. How could she even blame Rauf for his distrust when that fax had thrown up such seemingly convincing proof of her involvement in the matter of those missing funds? How could she blame him when she had yet to tell him the real truth about her relationship with Brett?

Possibly, Rauf had always sensed that he was not hearing the whole story and that was why he had stayed unconvinced. Yet what was the point of telling him now when they were parting? For of course they *had* to part; if Brett was to be prosecuted, if Rauf was to be protected from scandal, there was no option on that score.

So, she would hand herself over to the police, rather than wait for the police to catch up with her. Had she only fired off threats of divorce at Rauf because she was hurt and angry with him? When it came to crunch time, the thought of being without Rauf was like offering to have her heart removed without an anaesthetic. At the same time, when she thought of how proud Rauf was and how attached he was to his family, she could only cringe about how he must be feeling now at the knowledge that he had married a woman who could well be accused of criminal activity in the near future.

'I don't blame you for thinking I might be guilty,' Lily said miserably to Rauf as they walked through the airport at Istanbul. 'You had grounds—'

'No. No matter what life throws at me, I should *always* have faith in you—'

'How can you have when I come from a family who harboured Brett for so many years?' Lily mumbled, sunk in despair. 'It's better that we get a divorce and you just don't mention me to anyone. If your family was unhappy because you'd got married without them present, with a bit of luck they won't have discussed our marriage with any friends yet and it can all be hushed up.'

In a sudden move, Rauf closed a lean hand hard over hers as if divorce were so imminent he had to retain a bodily hold on her to prevent it. 'I've upset you a great deal but there is no reason whatsoever for you to be talking about divorce—'

'I don't think you'll feel that way if I'm arrested—'

'Should there be the slightest risk of that, I'll get you out of the country,' Rauf declared with a lack of hesitation that unnerved Lily, for it seemed to suggest that there was indeed a fair chance of such a situation developing. 'But as I will not be pressing charges against Gilman for the payments I didn't receive, that cannot happen—'

'But you really *wanted* to prosecute him—'

'You matter to me a great deal more than revenge,' Rauf confessed, brilliant golden eyes clinging to her delicate profile. 'Your peace of mind is also of paramount importance to me.'

Unwilling, it seemed, to cede him the ability to have even that amount of tender feeling for her, Lily sighed. 'Of course, you don't want to risk this whole horrible mess coming out in public and upsetting your family.'

In frustration, Rauf herded her into the waiting limousine.

'You can just take me to the police station and I'll get it all over with,' Lily muttered as he swung in beside her. 'It's not right that Brett should be let off—'

'It's not right that my wife should talk about divorcing me!' Rauf bit out rawly, tawny eyes shimmering over her startled face as he closed two strong hands round her tiny waist and propelled her toward him. 'Or that when you're innocent you should even consider approaching the police with a very complicated and confusing story which they might not understand as well as I do. Both subjects are closed. *For ever* closed—'

Held only inches away from him, Lily quivered, her tense body leaping with wicked immediacy to the proximity of his, her mind a bemused sea of anxious thoughts. '*But*—'

'Turkish wives don't argue with their men. Ask my

great-grandmother, Nelispah,' Rauf advised silkily. 'You can try to manipulate me in a thousand much more devious ways…that's OK, that's perfectly acceptable and even expected of you. But you *never* argue outright with me—'

'You quite like it when I argue with you—'

'Not on this issue, *güzelim*. Take it from me…I know best on this subject—'

'But when the police find out I'm a director in Harris Travel and Brett's prosecuted for what he did with those villas—'

'You're Lily Kasabian. You have done nothing wrong, therefore you can have nothing to fear,' Rauf murmured in a soothing and yet subtle forceful tone, striving to get through to her with every fibre of his extremely determined personality and seeing no reason to concern her with the reality that the police were already aware of her directorship in the firm. 'As my wife, your place is by my side and if any problems arise you can rest assured that *I* will move immediately to deal with them on your behalf.'

'I wish life was like that,' Lily mumbled, almost laughing in spite of her anxiety, for he really, truly believed that there was nothing he could not handle, nothing he could not make right.

'Life with me *is* and will be like that, I promise you,' Rauf intoned, golden gaze dropping to her sweet lush mouth, and then he tensed, fighting an almost irresistible urge to kiss her with all the pent-up passion that the mere mention of losing her had roused in him. *All you have ever wanted from me is sex*, however, was one of those Lily-type accusations calculated, Rauf knew, to come back and haunt him at the worst possible moments. The very last thing he wanted to risk was stoking that impression any higher. Tonight, when they went to bed in his riverside home, he would just *hold* her, nothing else. Maybe for at least a week he should hold her...

As if she were being tugged by elastic, Lily leant slowly forward in an inviting way, heart banging hard up against her ribs, lips tingling, but Rauf set her back from him with a preoccupied air. Truly embarrassed by her own disappointed expectations, Lily sank back into the far corner of the seat and endeavoured to concentrate instead on the exotic busy streets of Istanbul. Would everything be all right as he had sworn it would be? Ought she to listen to him? Then there was no point kidding herself that she wanted a divorce, was there?

Was he obsessed with sex? Rauf was engaged in a rare phase of the uneasy self-examination of the type that only overcame him in Lily's vicinity. He would have said he was obsessed with *her* but she had to have worked that out for herself by now. When a man married a woman within the space of four days, it was hardly a sign of sophisticated cool and restraint, was it? Especially when the same guy had spent all of his adult existence swearing that he was never, ever going to get married. Did Lily think sexual restraint was a demonstration of romantic and considerate caring even in marriage? Suddenly sexual restraint was looming on his horizon like a very big black cloud.

Apprehensive about meeting his family, Lily preceded Rauf into the enormous mansion where three generations of Kasabians lived. 'I bet you anything they don't like me—'

'Nelispah liked you on sight and my father will be very grateful that he won't have to listen ever again to the three of them bewailing the shame of me still being single,' Rauf informed her cheerfully.

From the minute the maid opened the door of the big, gracious drawing-room and Rauf's mother, Seren, a small, rounded brunette in her fifties emerged proffering an animated welcome in English, Lily did not have the time to be nervous. His father, a tall, craggier version of Rauf with greying hair, smiled at her. His grandmother, Manolya, was the quietest of the three older women. Nelispah Kasabian grasped Lily's hand in her frail fingers and just looked at her with tears in her bright old eyes and nodded to herself with satisfaction.

'You and I are to fly over to England tomorrow,' Rauf's father, Ersin, murmured to his son under the cover of the feminine chatter filling the room.

'Say that again,' Rauf invited.

'This promises to be a *very* traditional wedding,' Ersin stressed. 'We must ask Lily's father if he will accept you as a bridegroom—'

'He's already got me whether he likes it or not,' Rauf pointed out, inflamed by the prospect of being parted from Lily for even a day. On reflection, however, he conceded that he would not have dreamt of marrying one of his own countrywomen without first approaching her family. 'Yes, you're right. That is how it should've been done—'

'By the time you return alone to your own home this night, you will have discovered one of life's unhappier truths,' Ersin contended. 'Nelispah cannot be fought. She'll be upset if you argue and distraught if you refuse her expectations and how can you risk that?'

Rauf frowned. '*Alone*...what are you talking about?'

'If you're not ready to admit that you are already married, you can hardly be seen to take Lily into your home. I understood that you had agreed to that extraordinary arrangement on the phone last night—'

'Rauf...' From across the room, his great-grandmother was already stretching out a gnarled hand in greeting.

Go home alone without his wife? Were they all out of

their minds to ask such an outrageous thing of him? That wasn't a pound of flesh, that was an entire body they were demanding!

'Until we celebrate your wedding, Lily can stay here with us as if we are her family too. That way there will be no gossip,' the old lady told him happily.

Faint colour accentuated the tough slant of Rauf's high cheekbones and his hands clenched. He encountered his mother's pleading look of appeal and he compressed his lips on a surge of such anger at the idea of being separated from Lily that for an instant he could not trust himself to speak.

'You can visit Lily all the time,' his grandmother, Manolya, suggested in her usual anxious, placating fashion.

'But Rauf cannot be alone with her...otherwise people will say she is fast and we are too free,' Nelispah warned.

'Lily is already my wife,' Rauf said drily.

'You will have her all your life...but this is the time of betrothal, courting and bridal visits.' Nelispah spoke as though the entire process were on a calendar written in stone and ignored his reference to the civil ceremony. 'You will not want it said that you valued your bride so little that you would not follow custom or convention.'

Rauf breathed in very deep. 'What was customary over seventy years ago is—'

'The forty days and the forty nights,' his great-grandmother slotted in, making him turn pale. 'But we do not live in a village and, although I think it is sad that weddings must now be rushed affairs with less honour, I know a week must suffice.'

Even relieved of the threat of the forty days and nights, Rauf swallowed hard. A week. A week; seven days without Lily. He was aghast. But he looked down into the old lady's trusting, hopeful dark eyes and he knew that he had brought the situation on himself and that he could not, must not, hurt her any more than he already had with a blunt refusal. He jerked his proud dark head in grim acknowledgement and agreement. Ninety-nine per cent of the anguished tension holding the rest of his relatives rigid vanished at that point.

'I must explain this to Lily…in private,' Rauf murmured flatly.

'Leave the door open…' Nelispah urged after frowning over that request.

Lily had absorbed the byplay of that curious little scene without the remotest understanding of what was happening. Rauf's mother had kept on talking to her while watching Rauf with a wary air of pronounced strain. But now everyone *but* Rauf seemed happy and relaxed. His lean, strong features were brooding and taut.

Extending a lean hand to Lily in silent invitation, he led her into the room next door. 'What's wrong?' Lily hissed in an urgent whisper.

Rauf growled something raw in Turkish under his breath and strode over to the tall windows, wide shoulders emanating wrathful tension. 'I've been stitched up by a ninety-two-year-old punishment professional!'

'Sorry?'

Rauf expelled his breath. 'Last night, I heard you talking to Brett on the phone—'

'You…*did*?' Lily exclaimed, trying to recall what she had said, belatedly grasping yet another unfortunate factor that might well have contributed to the angry distrust with which Rauf had reacted to the discovery that her name was on that bank account set up by the other man.

'While I was thinking about that…the matriarchs phoned me and I *may*…I really don't remember…have given Nelispah the impression that I was willing to go through with another more traditional wedding to soothe the feelings I had offended,' Rauf advanced. 'She is refusing to acknowledge the civil ceremony, which means that she expects us to behave as if we are still single.'

Lily frowned in bewilderment.

'Which entails you remaining here under this roof *without* me until we are married for a second time,' Rauf extended grittily.

'Oh...*oh*!' Lily gasped. 'But that's ten days away—'

'A week—'

'No, your mother was quite clear about the date.'

'Nelispah is behaving as though our marriage in the civil ceremony was an elopement...*ayip*...something shameful!' Rauf ground out.

'I don't think so. She's very accepting of me and I'd hate to cause her pain.'

Rauf explained that he was flying over to her home the following day to visit her family.

'Oh, no...Hilary hates you!' Lily exclaimed in dismay.

Rauf watched Lily pin an embarrassed hand to her parted lips as she appreciated what she had let drop and he squared his big shoulders, brilliant golden eyes shimmering.

'Because of the way you dumped me three years ago,' she added with a rueful grimace.

Every sin he had ever committed was now coming back to haunt him, Rauf reflected with a fatalistic feeling.

'What about the villas...and all that?' Lily prompted worriedly. 'Hilary and Dad need to be told.'

'Yes,' Rauf acknowledged. 'I'll take care of that—'

'I should phone her—'

'Yes, but only tell your sister that we've got married—'

'*But*—'

'I'll handle the bad stuff with tact. I'm family now too.'

His lean, gorgeous face serious, Rauf reached for her hands and drew her close. 'When I get back, I'll take you out on that tourist trail you were supposed to be following and nobody can argue about that. That's your duty to your sister, who sent you over here, and a business necessity.' A slumbrous smile of satisfaction slashed Rauf's handsome mouth as he came up with those indisputable facts, calculated to impress even his great-grandmother, who would be unable to even conceive that Lily might either travel round alone or fail to fulfil a family obligation.

'I'm still going to miss you,' Lily confided unevenly.

Rauf suppressed a groan. 'I should be back within forty-eight hours...but all of a sudden that seems a long way away...why *is* that?'

Lily wrapped her arms round his neck and pressed into connection with his lithe, powerful frame. In the very act of claiming her lush mouth with hungry heat, Rauf heard a slight cough sound from the hall and he yanked his dark head up again, eyes a blaze of smouldering gold. 'The second wedding can't come fast enough for me, *güzelim*.'

The next twenty-four hours were very busy for Lily. When she phoned her sister, Hilary was stunned to be told that Lily was already married to Rauf, but mollified by the discovery that there was a second, more formal wedding yet to come. 'Of course, we'll come over for it. With a little luck, Rauf will send his private jet to fetch us and we'll save on the fares,' Hilary teased with considerable amusement. 'In return, I will desist from calling him a rat and endeavour to like him.'

Lily got on like a house on fire with Rauf's relatives and she was warmed by their affectionate lack of reserve with her. A large ceremonial tea party was held that afternoon and every female acquaintance of the Kasabian family appeared to be on the guest list. Lily was the centre of an admiring and curious throng. When Nelispah Kasabian became tired, Lily accompanied the old lady into another room where she lay down on a couch to rest for a while.

As Lily emerged again a beautiful brunette, garbed in an elegant white trouser suit, intercepted her to introduce herself. 'I'm Kasmet. I've known Rauf almost all my life...'

Lily smiled.

'But I was very surprised to hear that he was getting married,' Kasmet continued, sultry dark eyes bright with scorn. 'After all, he's still in love with me!'

Lily blinked in bemusement. 'I beg your pardon?'

'Of course, Rauf would never admit that...even when we had an affair earlier this year. He's too stubborn and proud,' the other woman informed Lily, her ripe mouth setting into a thinned line. 'But I want you to know it. I want you to *know* that you're second-best. He fell for me when we were teenagers and he never got over me.'

Blue eyes wide with astonishment, Lily spoke her own first thought out loud without meaning to do so. 'You must be the girl he caught with one of his friends!'

Infuriated coins of scarlet bloomed over Kasmet's cheeks.

'I'm sorry...I didn't mean to say that,' Lily mumbled, shaken by the other woman's spite, but also rather embarrassed by her own rejoinder.

Unexpectedly, Kasmet loosed a bitter laugh. 'I had too much to drink and I was foolish. I didn't love my late husband but because I lost Rauf, I married him. Could you really imagine my preferring any other man to Rauf?'

After that revealing little speech, Lily was pale and, reluctant to listen to any further revelations from the aggressive brunette, she murmured, 'Please excuse me...'

The afternoon continued but, from that point on, Lily

was challenged to play the part of the happy bride-to-be. Her mind was in turmoil. Oh, yes, she knew Kasmet had been angry and resentful and keen to cause trouble and pain. She wasn't stupid, was she? But the problem was that Lily also knew Rauf and the darker side of his forceful character. No, not even if he had expected to love Kasmet to the end of his natural life would Rauf have forgiven her infidelity. For that reason, Kasmet's assurance that she had had a recent affair with Rauf had upset Lily the most. For why would Rauf have got involved again with a woman who had once betrayed him? The answer to that question could only be that Rauf must still have had strong feelings for Kasmet.

For the very first time ever, it occurred to Lily that there might actually be a very good reason why Rauf had only ever talked of 'caring' for herself: if all along he had loved another woman. A woman he wouldn't marry. Although he had had an affair with Kasmet, he had ended that relationship as well. He had succumbed to temptation and then fought temptation off again, which was exactly how Lily could picture him behaving: at war with himself from start to finish. Her own heart had sunk to the soles of her feet. Somehow she had contrived to come to terms with the idea that Rauf didn't love her, but the wounding suspicion that he might feel much more for another woman savaged her.

Fresh from his successful manoeuvres in England, and having stopped off in Paris to do some necessary shopping on the way home, Rauf watched the staff struggling to cart the vast bulk of the carved *düzen* up the steps of his family home. Lily would be surprised and pleased that he was getting into the spirit of the occasion. In eight days, four-teen hours and thirty seven minutes, Lily would be back where she belonged by his side, in his home and in his bed. While he waited, he would use that time to demonstrate what a wonderful husband he could be: romantic, tender, caring, considerate, sensitive, generous, patient, magnanimous and tolerant. Having mentally scored a little tick beside each and every one of those desirable qualities in the performance of which he was certain he could excel, Rauf made his entrance and was relieved to find Lily alone.

'Lily…' he breathed with satisfaction.

'Rauf…' Lily feasted her shadowed blue eyes on him for one painful moment and managed a lacklustre smile. In a lightweight dove-grey suit cut to fit his lithe, wide-shouldered masculine physique by a master tailor with designer style, Rauf looked utterly breathtaking: sleek, sexy, gorgeous. There he lounged, the ultimate fantasy fix of masculinity, his face slashed by a vibrant smile that was capable of melting the skin off her bones…*but* Lily blocked him out in self-defence and wished her rapid heartbeat had as much pride.

'Miss me?' Rauf demanded.

'We've been very busy here…' Lily compressed her soft mouth. After all, it had taken Rauf *two* days to return to Turkey while his father had flown back after less than twenty-four hours away. But then, just as she should have known, she told herself wretchedly, if her body was out of bounds Rauf had been in no great hurry to get back to her and that had hurt. But was it fair for her to judge him on that? After all, who had tossed and turned every night just thinking about *him*? Thinking blush-making stuff too, Lily reminded herself guiltily, recalling the depth of her own longing for him and striving not to cringe where she sat.

At that point a welcome diversion was created by the entry of a staggeringly large wooden trunk adorned with ornate carving.

'The *düzen*…my first gift to you.' Resisting a dangerous urge to ask what was the matter with her, reminding himself that his former lack of faith in her had undoubtedly made her think less of him, Rauf opened the trunk and removed a large box from the interior.

'What's this?' Lily asked weakly.

'The fabric for your wedding dress…it's an old custom for the bridegroom to provide it—'

'I thought you weren't into customs…' Determined not to be impressed, Lily lifted the lid on the box. An exquisite expanse of fine gold hand-embroidered white silk was revealed. 'Oh…it's out of this world!'

'Don't let me see it—' Rauf warned as she almost cast aside the lid in her excitement.

'I thought you chose it—'

Rauf dealt her a discomfited look that tugged at her heart no matter how hard she tried to resist. 'Don't mention it to the diehard traditionalists in the household, but I want it to be a surprise when I see you in your wedding gown. I just listed what I thought you might dislike and left the choosing to the designer. She's flying in this evening for a dress fitting.'

Lily replaced the lid on the box and studied him with dreamy eyes because she found that confession so sweet. It was no use. She couldn't be cool with him when she just loved him to death. So maybe he did have a slight secret yen for the svelte, sophisticated Kasmet but she was not about to make the crucial error of questioning him on that score. Of course, Rauf had had at least one significant relationship and if she pried into his past he would resent it and what would she gain? Well, he would tell her the truth if she asked, only sometimes the truth could hurt, she acknowledged ruefully.

'I picked everything else in the trunk,' Rauf assured her.

'Everything else…?' Lily got up to look down into the trunk in amazement. It was packed full of clothes.

'Your trousseau…' Rauf regarded her with vibrant amusement. 'But I had the lingerie conveyed up to your room in a separate delivery. I didn't want to embarrass you—'

'You bought me lingerie…?'

'And what a very erotic experience that was, *güzelim*.' The smouldering undertone Rauf utilised made her mouth run dry and her face burn.

The tap-tap of his great-grandmother's stick warned that they were about to have company. Nelispah Kasabian's delight at the sight of that giant trunk was touching to behold.

'Of course, I'm being shortchanged here,' Rauf murmured silkily to Lily under cover of the chatter that erupted between their companions.

'How?'

'You're supposed to respond with the equivalent of a bottom drawer you've been industriously sewing and collecting up since childhood,' Rauf shared mockingly. 'Full of useful items like saddlebags and saucepans and hand-stitched sheets.'

'I'm afraid you're getting the equivalent of the barefoot bride,' Lily confided, dying to ask him how he had got on with Hilary but reluctant to do so with an audience around.

Half an hour later, Rauf took Lily in his car to see the sumptuous Topkapi Palace, the former residence of the Ottoman sultans for over four hundred years, out at Seraglio Point.

'So what happened with my sister and why hasn't she phoned me?'

'She said that she would prefer to talk to you when she comes over for the wedding—'

'Stop holding out on me…was she horribly upset about the villas?'

'Shocked and extremely angry. However, your father has agreed that I can buy into Harris Travel in the guise of an equal partner,' Rauf divulged. 'Hilary said no initially but I can be very persuasive.'

'Yes, I know…' Studying his bold bronzed profile, picking up on the quiet note of satisfaction in his dark, deep drawl, she smiled. 'You've been incredibly kind—'

'Your family has had a rough ride and I wanted to help—'

'Do you always get what you want?'

'You were one of my very few failures.'

'And Kasmet?' The other woman's name just leapt off Lily's tongue before she could prevent it.

At the traffic lights, Rauf turned with a frown to shoot her a piercing dark glance of enquiry. 'Where did you meet her?'

Lily coloured. 'She was at the tea party your mother held—'

Rauf grimaced. 'My father still does business with her father but I'm surprised she had the nerve to attend. None of us like her—'

'According to her, you're *still* madly in love with her.'

Rauf dealt her a thunderstruck appraisal. 'Eleven years after I caught her in bed with someone else?' he demanded in disbelief.

'Then I gather you didn't have a recent affair with her.' Lily was amused.

Car horns shrilled behind them as Rauf's stunned scrutiny flared into outrage. 'Are you out of your mind? She told you *that*? Right,' he ground out, nosing the sleek sports car with aggressive intent into another lane. 'I'm going over to her home to settle this now—'

'No…no, please, let's not do that!' Lily exclaimed in lively dismay.

'If she wants to tell lies, she can pay the price of being called on them!'

'I wouldn't give her the satisfaction—'

'Of knowing that you believed every word?' Rauf slotted in. 'You're my wife and I won't be slandered, nor will I allow anyone to upset you—'

'I'll be much more upset if you make a big thing of this!' Lily warned. 'I just wondered…that's all, but now I can accept that Kasmet was simply being spiteful—'

'After I've spoken to her, she won't indulge that spite around you again,' Rauf swore, untouched by her efforts to cool him down.

Never had Lily been so relieved as when Rauf hit the bell on a smart townhouse some minutes later and nobody answered the door. Extravagantly handsome features still set with fierce determination, he swung back into the car.

'I can't wait to see the Topkapi Palace…' Lily murmured placatingly.

Rauf looked at her, beautiful eyes molten gold, and then he leant over her, closed one hand into the silky fall of her pale hair and kissed her with a drugging, possessive fervour that electrified her sensation-starved body. She tipped her head back, heart hammering, heat burning between her slender thighs, opening her mouth to his, trembling at the hungry thrust of his tongue into the tender interior.

With a driven groan, Rauf jerked back from her, dragged in a shuddering breath. 'You see…I lose it with you. I can't even keep my hands off you in public places!'

'So let's go somewhere private,' Lily heard herself whisper without even thinking about it.

'No…no sneaking around,' Rauf spelt out, shooting the powerful car into reverse without looking back at her.

Lily had flushed to the roots of her hair. 'We're married!'

'We've got a lifetime ahead,' Rauf asserted grittily, resisting temptation with all his might.

An hour later, in the shade of the garden pavilion in the fourth courtyard of the palace, Lily gazed at the spectacular view of the sea but her thoughts were far away. She was thinking of the immediacy with which Rauf had responded to her questions about Kasmet and comparing his blunt honesty with her own secrecy about Brett. Time and time again, she had utilised weak excuses to persuade herself that she need not tell Rauf the unpleasant truth about Brett's behaviour towards her, but in only telling half of the story she had not been fair to either herself or Rauf.

Drawing in a slow, strengthening breath of the hot, still air, Lily said in sudden decision. 'I have something I want to tell you…I want you to understand why I've always been scared of Brett…. No, *please* don't interrupt me!'

In open disconcertion, Rauf made a sudden movement towards her, his frowning dark golden gaze probing her pale, taut face.

In the uneasy silence, Lily jerked a slim shoulder. 'I suppose it's an irrational fear but, the trouble is, he got to me when I was too young to know how to handle a bully like him,' she confided heavily. 'That first time I saw Brett with another woman and told Dad, Brett realised that it was me who had seen him. He picked me up at school and acted like a madman because he wanted to frighten me. He shouted at me and threatened me and he said if I ever talked about him again, he would tell Hilary that I'd been…you know…er…trying to come on to him…'

As a revealing look of revulsion entered her stricken

gaze in remembrance Rauf bit out something savage in his own language and reached for her knotted hands to take them in his. His big, powerful frame was rigid and the pallor of deep shock and anger was visible round the harsh set of his firm mouth.

'Even now, I don't know whether or not Hilary would ever have accepted my word against Brett's. She was crazy about him and she thought he was very handsome and was always saying how other women flirted with him. So I kept quiet but that wasn't enough for Brett. He hated me and he liked to make me squirm,' Lily muttered through compressed lips. 'For three years until I was able to leave home to go to college, Brett tormented me.'

'How?' The demand left Rauf like a bullet and his hands closed taut over hers.

'When there was nobody else within hearing, he'd make sick comments and stuff…' Lily grimaced and had to steel herself to continue. 'About how my body was shaping up…and crack dirty jokes…he never laid a hand on me but I was very scared that, some day, he *would*.'

Rauf closed supportive arms round her slight, shivering figure and eased her close. He himself was literally shaking with rage. He knew that if he ever got within twenty feet of Gilman, he would want to kill him. He snatched in a great, shuddering lungful of fresh air in an effort to get a grip on himself. What a blind fool he had been not to put what he already knew together and come up with a more likely scenario than Lily having been in love with her sister's husband! Now he knew what his former accountant, Tecer Godian, had been warning him about: the older man had seen Lily's fear of her brother-in-law.

'I didn't tell Dad because I was afraid that Brett might carry out that threat he'd made and say that *I* had been trying to tempt *him*. How could I prove that he was lying when the truth would have wrecked Hilary's marriage? Who was going to even *want* to believe me? I couldn't cope with the situation—'

'Of course you couldn't...' Rauf breathed in a fierce undertone. 'You should have told me about all this three years ago.'

'I was afraid you might think that I'd encouraged him and, anyway, keeping it all a secret was too much of a habit by then,' Lily confessed jaggedly. 'It was because of Brett that I started to dress the way I do—I was trying not to attract his attention. It was only when I went to college that I realised how different I was from other girls. I was so nervous around the boys...I didn't even like being looked at because that reminded me of Brett and it made me feel unclean.'

'It's all right...all right,' Rauf muttered thickly, attacked by a raw mixture of guilt and even fiercer regret for his own lack of understanding.

'But I fell in love with you, so I tried harder with you,' Lily admitted painfully. 'After you...well, a good while after you, I went for counselling because I knew it wasn't normal to feel the way I did.'

For a long time, Rauf just held her close. When the sound of voices warned that they were about to be disturbed, Rauf took her to the restaurant. At a quiet table on the garden terrace, he asked her about the counselling sessions she had attended.

'Realising that I was letting Brett ruin my life was the start of my recovery,' Lily said with a wry grimace. 'All that awful secrecy in my family, the trapped feeling I used to have in our home when he was around, the feeling of helplessness...that was what made me the way I was. I let Brett turn me into a victim—'

'I didn't help...' Rauf closed a hand over hers, his dark-as-midnight eyes overbright with unashamed pain at what she had endured. 'All along I sensed your reserve with me and it made me uneasy and too quick to ascribe other motives to your behaviour. But I did nothing to encourage your trust, *güzelim*.'

Her throat thickened and she swallowed hard. It felt good that there were no more secrets between them. He had not doubted her either; no, he had not doubted her for even a moment. A winging sense of joyous relief filled her, natural colour warming her cheeks again, any lingering tension banished.

The days that followed in the run-up to their wedding were a hive of constant activity. Having given her a whistle-stop tour of the main sights of Istanbul, Rauf whisked Lily off to the sites that lay further afield. She made initially nervous inroads into her new wardrobe and discovered that, although the clothes Rauf had chosen for her were a feast of designer style, none could be deemed either revealing or daring, and she teased him about the reality that his great-grandmother admired most of the outfits too.

Midweek, Rauf brought her the evidence of Brett's attempt to involve her in the fake bank account he had set up at that Turkish bank in London. Rauf had obtained a copy of the signature purporting to have been hers and the handwriting did not even bear the slightest resemblance to her own.

'A clumsy forgery which would fool nobody,' Rauf pronounced with satisfaction. 'Gilman believes that he's very clever, but he falls down on all the finer details.'

'Yes, but what's going to happen about him?' Lily asked anxiously.

'I don't want you to let a single thought of him enter your head.' His lean, dark features full of purpose, his dark golden eyes rested with concern on her troubled expression. 'Trust me. He will be dealt with. Never again will he be in a position to hurt you or anyone else in your family.'

By the end of that week, cheerfully anticipating her own family's arrival for the wedding festivities, Lily hugged an entire series of happy memories to herself and myriad impressions of the rich Turkish culture.

Visiting the exotic Spice Bazaar in Istanbul where the heady aroma of countless spices mingled in the air had been interesting, but walking hand-in-hand with Rauf had been a quieter and more private pleasure. The fascination of wandering round the amazingly intact ruins of the ancient city of Ephesus had been eclipsed by the preparation with which Rauf had ensured that he could answer her every question as well as any guide and his touching pride and love of the history of his own country.

She had done the tourist trail for her sister: she had bathed in the warm pools on the blinding white travertine terraces at Pammukkale, wandered through an astonishing underground city once inhabited by early Christians in Cappadochia and, at Dalyan, sailed alone with Rauf along the sleepy river bounded on all sides by swaying thickets of reeds. They lunched from a hamper in the shade of a chestnut tree and she listened to him tell her about childhood picnics, attended by anything up to seventy members of his extended family and still a favoured way of entertaining.

'You like picnics too…' Rauf made that reminder in a teasing undertone as he banded both arms round her to tug her into closer connection with his long, powerful frame, sending a chain reaction of intense awareness travelling through her. 'Only a very obstinate male would have fought the inevitable as long as I did. But I must confess that it is three years since I chose the diamond ring you wear on your finger.'

'Sorry?' Blue eyes wide, Lily met his burnished golden gaze in pure shock. 'You bought me an engagement ring *then*?'

'Yes…I intended to ask you to marry me that last weekend I spent with you in England,' Rauf confessed ruefully. 'But your niece, Gemma, was ill when we arrived and your father was preoccupied with that contract. Even I could see that it wasn't the right time to stage a romantic proposal…I expected to fly back to see you the following week.'

'And instead you saw me with Brett at the hotel and assumed the worst.' Lily was overjoyed that, in spite of their imperfect relationship three years earlier, Rauf had wanted to marry her even then, but she was also hurt that they should still have parted in misunderstanding and lost each other.

'I was too proud to confront you with my suspicions. I will regret that for the rest of my life,' Rauf admitted in a roughened undertone, his hard-boned, devastatingly handsome features taut. 'But the conviction that you could never have felt for me what I felt for you because you loved someone else made the most sense to me then. I was devastated…*too* devastated to judge the facts with intelligence or even keep them in proportion. To save face, I said nothing.'

'Oh, Rauf…' Lily whispered unsteadily, her gaze clinging to his remorseful gaze. 'Do all Turkish men have such colourful imaginations?'

'We're a passionate people. But, between you and I, the greatest weakness was that too much had been left unsaid,' Rauf conceded half under his breath, rational thought receding as he met her beautiful eyes and struggled to concentrate.

Electric tension hummed between them in the stillness of the grassy glade.

'Left unsaid…' Lily echoed, mouth running dry, a languorous, wanton heat infiltrating her with the desire that he could awaken so easily.

Rauf bent his dark head and kissed her just once in a stormy surge of pent-up hunger that made her quiver with almost painful longing. As he jerked back from her, releasing his breath in a stark exhalation at the cost of that restraint, she was tempted to haul him greedily back to her.

'In a couple of days, we'll be together again, *güzelim*,' he framed unevenly, catching her hand in his, pressing his lips to the centre of her palm. 'I want that to be special.'

They flew back to Istanbul in the helicopter that afternoon. At the airport, Rauf received a call informing him of a dispute at one of his newspapers. With a long-suffering groan, he tucked her into the limousine that would take her back to his family home while he went into the office to deal with the threatened strike. 'I might not be able to make it back in time to take everyone out for dinner as I promised,' he warned her ruefully.

He did not make it back in time and, although the rest of his family went ahead on their own, Lily was feeling tired and, aware that her own relatives would be arriving the next day, she decided to have an early night instead. After a light meal, she was about to do exactly that when a maid entered to tell her that she had a visitor. Every evening over the preceding week Lily had sat with the matriarchs and received formal visits and gifts of gold jewellery from the older generation of guests who would be attending their wedding. On this occasion, shorn of the helpful support of Rauf's family, Lily could only hope that her unlucky last-minute visitor spoke a little English.

But when she walked into the airy drawing-room the welcoming smile on her lips fell away as her aghast gaze landed on the tall, lanky blond man posed by the fireplace.

Brett gave her an unpleasant smile. 'Didn't I tell you I'd see you soon?'

CHAPTER TEN

FOR possibly the longest moment of her existence, Lily was frozen to the spot.

She stared back at Brett with a choking sensation of fear in her throat and goose-flesh prickling the nape of her neck. Yet even as she looked, incredulous that he should have taken the risk of not only coming to Turkey, but also daring to visit her at the Kasabian home, she was noting the changes in him. Usually a very sharp dresser, he was wearing a crumpled suit, he needed a shave and his pale blue eyes were bloodshot. As he moved forward she got a whiff of the sour smell of alcohol and recognised the ennervated edge of desperation he was striving to conceal.

'I know all the Kasabians are out tonight,' Brett told her in an effort to intimidate her. 'I watched them leave the house and I'm sure you'll want to keep this little courtesy call of mine to yourself.'

'And why would I want to do that?' Although Lily's own voice emerged faint in tone, she was already overcoming her old instinctive fear of him and seeing him with the eyes of a woman rather than a frightened teenager. The family might be out but the door onto the hall was still ajar and she knew that one of the staff would be hovering out there, waiting to receive the expected request for tea for her visitor.

'How could you think I would be dumb enough to credit that Rauf Kasabian had married you within a couple of days of your arrival here? Give me a break,' Brett mocked. 'The wedding of the year doesn't take place until the day after tomorrow. I was able to read that in one of Kasabian's own newspapers. But the wedding of the year *won't* take place at all if I start shooting my mouth off...'

In spite of the knowledge that she could have nothing to fear from Brett and that she and Rauf were already married, a cold, chilled sensation infiltrated Lily's stomach, a hangover from the bad old days when Brett had seemed to second-guess her at every turn. She wanted to call the police but realised that she did not even know what phone number she needed to use, nor how she could contrive to leave Brett alone without making him suspicious.

'Won't it?' Lily lifted her chin and studied him with loathing. 'You can't hurt me any more.'

An unattractive flush of colour mottled Brett's sallow skin. 'Can't I? Let me share a secret with you. Kasabian's cash payments on that contract were never made and, sooner or later, the news that that money has gone missing will emerge and all hell is going to break loose at Harris Travel. But if you tell Rauf about that now, you'll be in big trouble too.'

'I don't think so,' Lily countered drily without turning a hair in receipt of what Brett had evidently hoped would be a bombshell.

Brett's full mouth twisted. 'Well, that just proves how stupid you are, because when I set up another bank account to syphon those payments off I put *your* name on that account too! If I go down, I'll take you down with me. I'll say we had an affair and that you were in on the theft every step of the way with me. So, you'd better keep quiet until you get that wedding ring on your finger—'

'Still the same old threats and they're sounding very tired,' Lily cut in with angry contempt. 'You're not dealing with a scared little teenager now and I know *you* have to be very scared to have risked coming over here—'

'Go upstairs, Lily…' Another achingly familiar male voice intervened from behind her. 'I'll deal with this.'

In the seconds that followed Rauf's quiet entrance, Brett succumbed to panic. Surging forward just as Lily spun round in surprise and relief to see Rauf, Brett gave Lily a violent shove out of his path in an effort to reach the door and Rauf went for him like a lion. But Rauf only managed to land one powerful punch on the other man before registering that Lily, who had been smashed up against the wall, had fallen. Rauf's rage that Gilman should have dared to approach his wife with threats again was overpowered by his fear that Lily might have been seriously hurt.

Dizzy and winded by that fall, Lily was gathered with anxious care into Rauf's arms and lifted over to the nearest couch. 'Are you all right?' he demanded rawly.

'Brett?' she gasped.

The slam of the front door answered that query and Rauf groaned out loud in frustration. 'I came back minutes after he arrived and I called the police immediately. I should've stayed out of the room until they arrived but I couldn't *stand* to hear him threatening you!'

'I'm just glad he's gone,' Lily confided unevenly.

Thinking that having Gilman arrested and charged just before their wedding might have cast something of a pall over the festivities, Rauf just held her close and wished he had contrived to get more than one healthy punch in.

'And I'm so grateful there wasn't a fight,' Lily added.

Again, Rauf said nothing, knowing that she would be dismayed by the admission that he felt seriously deprived of what had very probably been his one and only opportunity to pulverise the vicious little creep. He ushered Lily upstairs to her room and then went back down to deal with the police.

Lily's family arrived the following afternoon. Douglas Harris looked brighter than he had in months and her three nieces were bubbling over with excitement. After a slew of necessary introductions and socialising and talking to her father, who was full of praise for Rauf, Lily took Hilary into another room so that they could talk in private.

Her sister enveloped her straight into an unusually emotional hug before sighing. 'I didn't phone because I had too much to tell you. For starters, this week I heard that Brett and my erstwhile friend, Janice, had split up.'

'Oh...good,' Lily pronounced. 'That's justice.'

'Well, it may *well* be.' Hilary gave her a wry scrutiny. 'Apparently, Brett has done something dishonest with Janice's divorce settlement and the police are involved there too. There's a rumour that he's been gambling—'

'Gambling?'

'I suspect that explains what he did with all the cash he helped himself to from Harris Travel,' Hilary said with fierce resentment. 'But I can be grateful for two things... one, that Brett has been such a useless father that the girls won't ever miss what they've never had, and two, thank goodness, I wised up to what a louse I'd married years ago!'

Lily blinked at that blunt and surprising assurance. 'You... *did*?'

'Unfortunately, I hadn't the slightest idea that he couldn't be trusted with money,' Hilary conceded heavily. 'But just before Joy was born I realised that he was running round with other women. By then, though, Dad had gone and signed over the house and that and the girls made me feel that I had to try and keep our marriage together—'

'I can understand that, but if you didn't love Brett any more why did you always look so sad after the divorce whenever he was mentioned?' Lily prompted.

Her older sister winced. 'Put that down to the awful knowledge that I've wasted the last few years of my life. I just got on with being a mother and I turned a blind eye to Brett's affairs. If I had ever dreamt what was *really* going on under my own stupid nose, if I had known that, way before you even left school, Brett was threatening you...' she breathed painfully and slowly shook her head with bitter regret '...I'd have slaughtered Brett long ago!'

Thrown by that declaration, for Lily had still had no plans to tell her sister quite how low her ex-husband had sunk in the more distant past, Lily exclaimed, 'How did you find out?'

'Rauf brought me up to date and, no, don't you dare criticise him for interfering because I just know that you weren't *ever* going to tell me!' Hilary admitted ruefully. 'And after finding out about that, learning that my ex-husband is on the run from the Turkish police didn't phase me at all. If I knew where Brett was, I'd hand him over personally—'

'Are you serious?' Lily interrupted, for she had been wondering how on earth they would cope if Brett was caught before the wedding and had feared that her sister would be very distressed by any such development.

'I want him prosecuted and locked up too.' Hilary breathed in deep, her fine features rigid and flushed with anger. 'In fact, when Rauf told me about Brett having the neck to come here last night and try his old tricks on you, my blood just boiled!'

The sisters talked for over an hour and then Lily finally asked Hilary what she thought of Rauf.

'He just adores you. It shines out of him like a light,' Hilary quipped with sudden amusement. 'Why are you

looking surprised? I mean, you've got to know that after
he hauled you off to the altar so fast. I couldn't believe
it!'

He adores you. Lily almost mentioned that Rauf had
rushed into that civil ceremony primarily out of a wish to
protect her reputation, but thought better of it because she
could see that Hilary was charmed by the belief that she
was on the sidelines of a true romance. Rauf was warm,
tender, romantic and everything she had always known he
could be, but he had yet to mention that word 'love' and
Lily was already so happy that she was determined not to
let that bother her.

At dawn the following morning, the pre-wedding prep-
arations began. Lily was ushered out to the *hamam*,
wrapped in a sturdy sarong and, surrounded by animated
women, whisked through the entire invigorating process of
being warmed, cooled down again by playful scoops of
cool water tossed over her and then enveloped in loads of
bubbles from head to toe and scrubbed by a lady built like
a human tank with an abrasive mitt. It was fun and Lily
giggled a lot. Finally rinsed clean while Hilary looked on
in awe, Lily's hair was subjected to a camomile bath that
left the strands as sleek and glossy as pure silk, and she
was settled onto a couch where she was massaged with
fragrant oil. Far from it being the over-vigorous process
she had feared, it was very relaxing.

In the outer room, she was served with apple tea and
her nails were manicured before an elaborate henna pattern
was painted onto her right hand. 'To soothe Nelispah,'
Rauf's mother whispered, explaining that the old lady had
been a little disappointed to be told that Lily would not be
entering the hotel ballroom, where the wedding would be
celebrated, on the back of a white horse.

A couple of hours later, Lily pirouetted in front of a
full-length mirror, hopelessly in love with her gorgeous

wedding gown. The simple traditional design she had selected made the most of the exquisite fabric. An elaborate and beautiful gold necklace arrived from Rauf as a bride gift and Nelispah's bright gaze shone as much as Lily's at that evidence of custom being observed. Beneath her gown, Lily wore a blue satin garter that Hilary had given her as well as the raciest set of silk lingerie in her possession and when her nieces, Penny, Gemma and Joy, danced in to surprise her with their pretty bridesmaids' dresses she was delighted.

She left the Kasabian home on her proud father's arm to climb into an open carriage drawn by two white horses. But without a doubt the moment that was the highlight of her day was when she entered the opulent hotel and saw Rauf waiting for her. He just stared with such blatant appreciation that she blushed, her own gaze equally absorbed in taking in how drop-dead gorgeous her husband looked in a superb dark suit.

'You take my breath away, *güzelim*,' he confided huskily, dark golden eyes possessive as the wedding march was played and he led her into the ballroom with their families and all the guests trooping in behind them.

The ceremony over, they ate a meal that began with the official wedding soup and afterwards they cut the cake and offered it round to their relatives. Rauf claimed a kiss at that point that sent her heartbeat racing.

'I wasn't expecting that,' she confided breathlessly as he whirled her out onto the floor to begin the dancing.

'Perfectly acceptable at our wedding.' His brilliant smile warmed her like the bright clear Turkish sunlight. 'But don't be surprised when I disappear later. My family bring my bride to the very door of my home and then we get a month's break from the whole lot of them—'

'I *love* your family!' Lily protested.

'Tomorrow we set off on our honeymoon cruise round the coast on my yacht,' Rauf imparted with satisfaction. 'And if we get tired of that, we can go anywhere, do anything—'

'Or sneak back to Sonngul,' Lily whispered. 'It still feels like my favourite place in the world.'

Her own family were staying on for a week's vacation with Rauf's family and Lily parted from them with farewell hugs to be borne off in a limousine containing Nelispah and Manolya, for the bridegroom's mother was not allowed to play a part in delivering the bride to her future home.

Set down before yet another ancient and huge house where Rauf awaited her, Lily laughed as he swept her off her feet and carried her indoors. 'It's been a wonderful, wonderful day,' she told him happily.

'It's not quite finished yet.' Rauf set her down with pronounced care and guided her into a glorious light-filled bedroom that overlooked the very waters of the Bosphorus. 'Do you know that I have never said the words, "I love you" to any woman and even today I feel ashamed to offer you my love?'

'*Ashamed?*' Lily studied him in shaken disbelief.

'But my love is yours, for what it is worth, and it *always* has been,' Rauf proclaimed tautly, lodged by the French windows that opened out onto a deck festooned with tubs of beautiful flowers.

'Always has been...' Lily parrotted, mesmerised by the sight of Rauf struggling to find words that were so obviously difficult for him to speak, scarcely able to even think about what he was telling her.

'At nineteen, I was infatuated with Kasmet, but I never knew love until I met you. She only hurt my pride and gave me an excuse to say marriage wasn't for me,' Rauf murmured grimly. 'You know, I'm still very angry about her telling you those ridiculous lies this week.'

'Forget about that. She was just envious and wanting to spoil my happiness,' Lily said dismissively, far more interested in what he had admitted just a minute earlier.

'Three years ago, when we first met, I was a slick operator or, at least, I *thought* I was.' His wide, sensual mouth twisted with a derision directed at himself. 'I wanted you on my terms and you were worthy of much more, but success with too many other women had made me arrogant and selfish. My obstinate belief that I would never marry almost destroyed our relationship—'

'You still bought that diamond ring I wear back then,' Lily reminded him gently, her blue eyes soft with love.

Dark colour accentuated his fabulous cheekbones. 'I was still immature. The ring would have been given then with a certain amount of resentment that I could win you no other way,' he admitted heavily. 'That is nothing to be proud of either. But this time around, from the outset of our first meeting, I was even worse—'

'How?'

'I was just eaten by jealousy of Gilman. I thought you were only in Turkey because he had taken off with another woman. When I realised you were a virgin, I was shattered, but that bitter jealousy was so ingrained in me after three years that I just moved on to suspecting that, even though you hadn't had an affair with him, you *had* loved him. Those first couple of days we were together, I acted like a guy with only one not very reliable brain cell.'

'You were jealous of Brett—?'

'And then when I heard you on the phone to him, I suffered the tortures of feeling second-best all over again. I needed to hear nothing suspect in the conversation to torment myself even more.' Rauf groaned.

'Yet, in spite of all that, you *still* wanted to marry me and you knew that you loved me.' Lily worked out those facts for herself with immense satisfaction, for that was a level of love she had never dreamt a male with his fierce pride could feel for her. That was love in block capitals, a love big enough and generous enough to overcome every obstacle and his pride as well.

'Then I blew it again on our flight to Istanbul over your name being on that bank account and there was nothing more sobering than realising that I was losing you altogether.' Rauf swore and spread speaking hands expressively wide.

'I'm not so easy to lose,' Lily confided.

'My pride made me persuade myself three years ago that my love for you had died,' he confessed tautly. 'But I know now that you genuinely cared for me in those days and that I must have hurt you a great deal...'

'Yes...you hurt me terribly,' Lily told him honestly.

Rauf paled but reacted much as if he had expected to have that confirmed.

'One minute you were there and the next it was like you'd never existed and I started to believe that I'd just imagined that we'd ever shared anything worth holding onto,' Lily continued. 'I decided it could only have been a casual thing for you—'

'*Casual?*' Rauf loosed a bitter laugh of disagreement. 'It was six months before I could even catch sight of a blonde head in the street without secretly, crazily hoping it would somehow be you. I worked myself into the ground that entire year, because at least when I was working it took my mind off you for a while. I never believed in love like that until I was without you and the hardest thing for me to accept now is that I deserved to be miserable.'

Lily was over the moon to learn that Rauf had had such

a hard time getting by without her, but thought it tactful to conceal a delight that struck her as a little cruel. At the same time she was now quietly rejoicing in his staggering assurance that his love was hers and always had been. 'I wasn't exactly happy myself. Tell me, when did you decide that you were still in love with me?'

'I always knew it was there deep down inside me…lurking…' Rauf expelled a heavy sigh. 'But I didn't ever think about it after the first year we were apart. I just shut it out until I saw you again. I went haywire and made appallingly bad decisions—'

'Such as?' Lily probed in growing fascination as she tried to think of love as something that 'lurked' like a secret, dreadful threat.

'I told myself that I was taking revenge when I took you to Sonngul to stay with me but, in truth, I was only snatching at the first possible excuse to be with you again. I didn't know what I was doing…not *really* doing until it was too late. But I knew I loved you at the civil ceremony—'

'So why didn't you mention it…why wait until now?'

'I had treated you with dishonour and that shamed me. I had not valued you as I should have done. I had even less right to be talking about love. All I had done was cause you more distress and I regret that most of all.'

'But I brought a lot of that on myself,' Lily countered guiltily. 'I couldn't make myself tell you what I'd had to put up with from Brett—'

'I could see that you were hiding something from me. You're not a very good dissembler,' Rauf told her gently. 'Once I knew that there was a secret, my suspicions about the nature of your relationship with him refused to die. Yet the moment I heard the truth that was the end of them.'

Lily flushed. 'Honesty pays,' she muttered in discomfiture.

'But an atmosphere of suspicion and distrust does not encourage honesty.' Rauf studied her with marked strain in his gleaming gaze, lean, strong face clenched taut. 'All I want to ask you now is if some day you feel you could love me again?'

Lily screened her gaze, not wanting to let him off the hook too fast. 'Anything's possible.'

'I love you enough for both of us, *güzelim*.'

'I'm really beginning to believe that you do.' Lily crossed the room to where he stood so straight and tall and, meeting the loving intensity of his tawny eyes, she just couldn't keep him in suspense any more. 'But luckily for both of us, I wasn't any better at getting over you than you were at getting over me...I'm still very much in love with you.'

For several seconds, Rauf stared back at her in surprise and then, all of a sudden, he strode forward and just snatched her into his arms with an extreme lack of cool. He curved unsteady hands to frame her cheekbones. 'You're not just saying that to save face for me?' he probed tautly.

'No, I'm not that kind,' Lily declared with eyes brimming with amusement at that very Turkish suggestion. 'I just love you lots and lots and never met anyone who could make me feel as you could.'

'Must be a lot of real losers out there because I wasn't that impressive,' Rauf muttered, and then he claimed her mouth with all the passion of his volatile temperament.

Matters moved fast from that point. Curtains were hastily yanked shut, clothes fell away without ceremony and the bride and groom fell between the sheets of the marital bed to make up for ten nights of being kept apart.

'I've been up walking the floor every night this week…I just missed you so much!' Rauf confided raggedly.

In between frantic kisses, Lily hugged that sense of security to herself, revelled in his hungry tenderness, the sheer happiness that she saw in his eyes. There was a new dimension to their loving, a wonderful closeness and contentment in the aftermath.

Rauf told her about Talip Hajjar's visit to Sonngul and how complete his faith had been in her that evening when he had explained to the army police officer what she was doing in Turkey. Then he made her laugh out loud as he admitted that the sight of her name on that bank account with Brett's had, within minutes of his angry condemnation of her, put him in a literal panic on her behalf.

'I immediately lost all desire to press charges against Brett because I was afraid the police would not be able to prove your innocence,' Rauf stated in some embarrassment. 'About then, I realised that I would lie for you, break the law, do absolutely *anything* required to protect you and that shattered my view of myself as an honourable man.'

Lily looked up into the dark golden eyes resting on her with adoring intensity and kept quiet rather than tell him that, next to those words of love that she had convinced herself that she would never hear, that was the most touching admission she had ever heard. 'I *was* a bit disconcerted when you suddenly mentioned getting me out of the country as if I was a master criminal!' she confided with a helpless giggle.

'I hadn't yet even laid charges against Brett for those missing funds, so how *could* you have been at any risk? I was functioning on that single brain cell again,' Rauf groaned incredulously. 'I think I know why I never fell in love before…ESP must've warned me it was likely to be the most humbling and embarrassing experience of my life.'

As he smoothed down her tumbled hair and welded her to his lean, relaxed length Lily smiled with sunny contentment. 'But I'm your reward…and, let's face it, humility never used to be one of your more marked traits,' she teased with new confidence. 'I love you all the more for just being you.'

'Flaws and all?'

Lily nodded forgivingly.

His shimmering smile curved his handsome mouth and warmed her all the way down to her toes. 'You're the best thing that ever happened to me…I love you more than anything else in this world.'

Twenty months later, Lily settled her infant son, Themsi into his canopied cot at Sonngul. Themsi was four months old. She hummed his favourite lullaby half under her breath until his big eyes slowly slid shut and the extravagant dark lashes he had inherited from his father drifted down onto his rounded little cheeks.

From the window of the nursery, she watched the sun go down in spring splendour over the beautiful gardens before she drew the curtains and walked back to check that her baby was as comfortable as he could be. Themsi was only just beginning to sleep in more than fits and snatches and she smiled at the memory of finding Rauf beating her to his first cry those initial broken nights, for nobody had fallen harder for Themsi at first glance than his father. Her son was a very much indulged baby. Nelispah Kasabian had wept over him in joy and her own daughter and granddaughter were equally enchanted with the new addition to the family.

'Four children?' Nelispah had whispered conspiratori-

ally to Lily, her wise old eyes fixed with satisfaction to
Rauf as he'd cradled his son with tender pride for a family
photograph. 'He's good for at least six! He's all heart un-
derneath the tough front.'

Yes, Lily had discovered that learning the Turkish language had paid definite dividends. Nelispah Kasabian
knew Rauf back to front and inside out but would never
have dreamt of revealing that fact to him.

Lily could barely believe that she had already been married for a year and eight months. The time had flown because she had never been happier. However, when Rauf
and Lily had returned from their wonderful honeymoon
they had been stunned to learn that Brett Gilman was dead.
Soon after Brett had contrived to get himself back to
England, he had been killed in a car accident. Apparently,
he had been drunk, but mercifully no other car had been
involved in the fatal crash. The files on Brett's criminal
activities had been closed.

Hilary had been stunned when her ex-husband had been
killed and the children had been very upset. At the same
time, Lily's nieces had seen so little of their irresponsible
father since the divorce that they had not been as badly
affected as they might have been. Rauf had tried to persuade her sister to allow him to buy her a larger home,
but her sister had said no. Hilary had been working hard
to build up Harris Travel again and Serhan Mirosh, the
quiet but very attractive forty-year-old investment consultant whom Rauf employed, had made increasingly frequent
visits to offer his advice and guidance.

Rauf had given Lily a wicked grin of satisfaction one
evening when he'd come home. 'Serhan has fallen in love
with Hilary. He sees her as a damsel in distress and longs
to take all her business burdens onto his own shoulders—'

'I don't believe you!' Lily laughed for Serhan had always struck her as a real sobersides for all his good looks.

Rauf's grin merely grew wider. 'He confessed this afternoon when he asked if I would have any objection to him taking your sister out to dinner. It might take him another month to work up the courage. He's very shy with women...why do you think he's still single?'

'I know Hilary likes working with him,' Lily conceded with a reflective frown. 'But she doesn't seem to have the slightest interest in meeting another man.'

'Serhan may be shy but he's also very determined when he sets his sights on something. If he's got anything to do with it, they'll be married within the year,' Rauf forecast with brazen confidence.

Lily had been overjoyed when Rauf's optimistic conviction had come true, although it had taken a little longer than a year for Serhan to get Hilary as far as the altar. His virtually proposing on the first date had been more of a hindrance than a help to his own cause. Just a month ago, however, Rauf and Lily had flown over to their wedding and had brought Penny, Gemma and Joy back home with them while the bridal couple had gone off on their honeymoon. Harris Travel had been sold and Hilary was planning to set up business again in Istanbul. Hilary had at last found the happiness she deserved and Lily was delighted that her sister and her daughters were now living nearby. Although pressed to take up residence with Serhan and Hilary in Turkey, Douglas Harris had decided to remain in England with his friends and all that was familiar and had moved into a comfortable flat in a retirement home.

Lily and Rauf came to Sonngul to unwind in peace and privacy whenever they could. Rauf strolled into their bedroom, his jacket slung over one broad shoulder, tie already loosened, and his dark golden eyes glittered with appreciation over the picture Lily made in her aqua-coloured nightdress. 'You look ravishing.'

'You're easily impressed,' Lily teased, but then if that was true she was a pushover on the same score: his lean, dark features and the lithe flow of his well-built physique set her heart jumping too.

'No, anything but. Every time I look at you, I know how lucky I am,' Rauf quipped as he went into the adjoining room, where Themsi always slept when they stayed at Sonngul, to have a look at his sleeping son. 'He's practically growing in front of our eyes,' he said fondly. 'He's going to be tall like me.'

Lily watched him from the doorway with amusement.

Rauf swung round. 'What's so funny?'

'I doubt that Themsi's had a growth spurt since you flew out of here this morning!'

Her tall, dark, handsome husband just closed his arms round her and lifted her right off her feet. 'He just might have had,' he told her stubbornly, and then he kissed her with passionate hunger, making her senses sing before conceding, 'but I suppose it's unlikely.'

Lying back on their bed, Lily reached up to tug him down to her again and smiled up into his clear golden eyes, loving every angle of his lean, strong face, rejoicing in their closeness and contentment.

'I hate being dragged away from you and Themsi when I'm here,' Rauf confided huskily. 'I'm going to set up a better office so that I can handle more on the spot.'

'Brilliant idea,' Lily told him.

A slashing smile curved his handsome mouth. 'I have my moments, *güzelim*.'

Lily gave him a mischievous look. 'Most days…why do you think I love you so much?'

He gazed down at her with amusement and love mingled in his possessive gaze. 'I adore you and you know it.'

And she *did* know that she was loved and, more than anything else, that security and confidence had added to her contentment. She found his mouth for herself and surrendered to the pleasure of their loving.

The world's bestselling romance series.

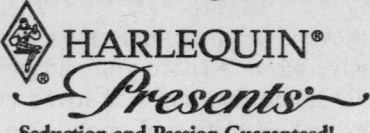

HARLEQUIN®
Presents~

Seduction and Passion Guaranteed!

Secret Passions

A spellbinding series by
Miranda Lee

Desire changes everything!

Women are always throwing themselves at Justin McCarthy—
picturing themselves spending his millions and cuddling up to
his perfect physique! So Rachel is Justin's idea of the perfect P.A.—
plain, prim and without a predatory bone in her body. Until a
makeover unleashes her beauty and unexpected emotion....

AT HER BOSS'S BIDDING
Harlequin Presents, #2301
On-sale February 2003

**Pick up a Harlequin Presents® novel and you will enter
a world of spine-tingling passion and provocative,
tantalizing romance!**

Available wherever Harlequin books are sold.

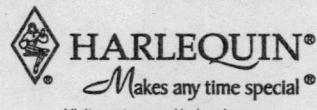

HARLEQUIN®
Makes any time special ®

Visit us at www.eHarlequin.com   HPSPMLF

The world's bestselling romance series.

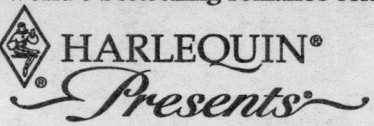

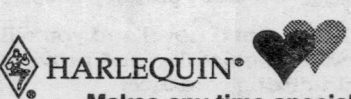

The world's bestselling romance series.

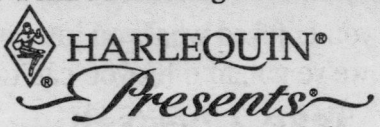

HARLEQUIN®
Presents

Seduction and Passion Guaranteed!

He's impatient… He's impossible…
But he's absolutely irresistible!
He's…

HER ITALIAN BOSS

Two original short stories to
celebrate Valentine's Day, by
your favorite Presents authors,
in one volume!

The Boss's Valentine by Lynne Graham

Poppy sent Santiano Aragone a Valentine card to cheer
him up. Santiano responded by making love to her…
and suddenly Poppy was expecting her boss's baby!

Rafael's Proposal by Kim Lawrence

Natalie's boss, Rafael Ransome, thought she couldn't be a
single mom and do her job. But then he offered her a
stunning career move—a Valentine's Day marriage proposal!

HER ITALIAN BOSS
Harlequin Presents, #2302
On-sale February 2003

**Pick up a Harlequin Presents® novel and you will
enter a world of spine-tingling passion and
provocative, tantalizing romance!**

Available wherever Harlequin books are sold.

HARLEQUIN®
Makes any time special ®
Visit us at www.eHarlequin.com

HPVCLG